CHRISTMAS TAPESTRY

CHRISTMAS TAPESTRY

A COLLECTION OF HOLIDAY TALES

KENNETH ANDRUS WILLIAM BERNHARDT

ROBERT A. BROWN TAMARA GRANTHAM

BETSEY KULAKOWSKI JOHN WOOLEY

EDITED BY
WILLIAM BERNHARDT

BABYLON
BOOKS

CONTENTS

INTRODUCTION

I've always loved Christmas—the holiday, the season, the spirit, the core concept that people all around the world can set aside their differences for a time and remember that we are all here to love one another. So the idea of gathering some of my favorite friends and authors for a holiday-themed anthology appealed to me. The question was how to do it with scribes of wildly different books—thrillers, paranormal suspense, fantasy, and horror—some of which do not normally lend themselves to seasonal sentimentality. I made the assignment even more daunting when I asked them to involve their series characters. But of course, with gifted writers, anything is possible.

Betsey Kulakowski leads the collection. Her television adventure-show host Lauren Grayson regularly tracks down the world's greatest paranormal mysteries, so it's only natural that this time she should be on the trail of Krampus. Tamara Grantham gives us a taste of her forthcoming Warrior Kingdoms fantasy world—during winter solstice—and the ongoing conflict between dragon riders and magicians. Robert

A Brown and John Wooley may have had the greatest challenge —writing a Christmassy story in *The Cleansing*'s 1930s horror universe—but they rose to the challenge beautifully. Kenneth Andrus put his espionage agent Nick Parkos to work obstructing a foreign power's plan to create super-soldiers. And I contributed a tale with Kenzi Rivera from my *Splitsville* legal thrillers using her sleuthing skills to help a friend's family rediscover the meaning of Christmas.

So grab the eggnog, kindle the Yule log, spin some Christmas tunes, and settle in for a good read. It's the season of miracles, my friends. And what could be more miraculous than a good book?

Enjoy.

William Bernhardt, Editor

CHAPTER I

THE KRAMPUS CONSPIRACY

BY BETSEY KULAKOWSKI

T he priest pulled his cloak up around his neck as the icy wind billowed up under his cassock. The cold wasn't entirely the result of the winter wind. An eerie sense of dread had chilled him to the core. It wasn't just that the night had gone foul. He'd been called out by one of his parishioners whose child had been attacked in the woods; a child who now lay on death's door. Last Rites were not traditionally performed upon children. If a child had never sinned or was too young to even understand what sin was, it made the Apostolic Pardon unnecessary for a child. But anointing of the sick, and comfort for their grieving parents, was something he could do, if he got there in time. Canon law forbade the anointing of the sick once life began to wane.

Father Johan Bernard might have been there sooner had his car not skidded off the road and become stuck in a snowdrift. Determined to reach the remote village, he'd had no choice but to attempt the journey on foot for the last few miles. He knew the way. He had made this journey many times; night, and day. He was the only priest in the parish assigned to tend the flock of this small hamlet in the *Schwarzwald*.

While he had been raised in Berlin, this region of Germany was isolated; it's people painfully superstitious. The father of the injured child had frantically rambled on about the child having been attacked by a beast, a beast that appeared as the dark harbinger of Saint Nicholas; a horrid creature known by the name Krampus. While a doctor lived in the village and would do what he could for the child, the father begged for the priest to come and pray for the child's immortal soul. Johan Bernard had heard of such legends, but he was more likely to believe in the Easter Bunny. He was an educated man.

A mournful scream echoed in the trees, and the priest froze, crossing himself. On nights like this, he was a little more willing to believe in dark forces. He tried to convince himself it was the wind as he pushed his way through the dense forest. The snow was now deeper than his boots. The icy flakes worked their way into his socks where they melted. As his socks grew wet, the cold intensified, and as the howl echoed again in the wind, the priest's speed increased.

As the growling grew louder, the priest became frantic until he moved at a lumbering pace; a desperate sprint through the almost knee-deep drifts. He wove through the trees when he lost the path to the village. His breath came in heavy gasps; clouds that clung around him as he ran, blinded by the snow that came in heavy waves. Droplets of ice clung to his thin lashes. A limb caught his stocking cap, tearing it from his head. Heedless of all else, he wove through the brambles, working his way up the rise of a hill, pausing with relief as the soft glow of a lamp in a distant window appeared; his saving grace.

He leaned heavily on his knees, feeling foolish for being afraid of the howling wind. He paused to catch his breath, leaning over to draw in great gulps of the cold air. What he saw on the ground in front of him though, made his heart stop. It missed several beats, and his head spun from the sudden lack of blood flow.

The footprints in the snow before him were massive, four times larger than a man's print. They looked like a man's print, except for the cockeyed little toe that jutted off to the side. They were deep too. The gap between the prints suggested the creature that made them was large with a long stride. Before his curiosity could be sated, a deep grumble came from behind him, and the priest froze. He turned without thinking and regretted it at once.

"*Mien Gott,*" he barely had a chance to mutter the words. A massive claw struck him before he could make the sign of the cross. The blow hit him on the side of the head, so hard flesh tore and blood flew from the wound. The crimson stained the pristine snow as the priest pulled himself up to his hands and knees. He would crawl if he needed to. He had to get away. But it was already too late. As the beast crouched, preparing to pounce, Bernard knew the hour of his death and did the only thing he could think to do.

He cowered, fumbling in his pocket with a trembling hand. The beast moved closer, growling deep in its chest. Its fetid breath was hot on his frozen skin. He lifted the rosary in his defense and began to pray. The demon seemed to recoil, and the priest became certain he had found his salvation. He raised his trembling voice, "*Gegrüßet seist du, Maria, voll der Gnade, der Herr ist mit dir. Du bist gebenedeit unter den Frauen, und gebenedeit ist die Frucht deines Leibes, Jesus ...*"

He never reached the *Amen.*

~

"Can't we just skip this who fiasco and go home?" Lauren sneered as the limo approached the museum where the evening's festivities were scheduled to take place.

"We've traveled an awful long way for this," Rowan said. "Not to mention the last five hours you spent getting ready. And you do look beautiful, so no. We're going out on the town."

"Yeah, well, you don't have plastic boning cutting into your rib cage," Lauren muttered, tugging on the side of her dress.

"I promise, I'll help you out of it later," he said, leaning down to kiss her bare neck. "Just try and relax. Let's enjoy this."

Rowan was right, it had been a long trip to get here. Three days ago, they'd been exploring Mahendraparvata, a recently discovered archeological site in the Phnom Kulen mountains of Northern Cambodia. Tonight, they were honored guests at the *International Society of Modern Scientists* Annual Awards Gala in Paris.

Over the past three days they'd flown from Phnom Penh to Kuala Lampur where they had a five hour layover. The next leg of their journey took them to Abu Dhabi where they'd had spent ten hours in the VIP lounge. Lauren had found a quiet place to catch a cat nap while Rowan checked emails and reviewed video from their expedition.

"I hope they'll have coffee," she said, out of nowhere.

"No champagne?"

"Coffee," Lauren repeated. "Strong. Sweet. Creamy."

The City of Lights offered a comforting glow. The Eifel Tower was barely visible as the freezing rain turned to snow.

The back of the limo was warm. Still, Lauren shivered as a chill ran down her arms. She tucked them up under the wrap.

He snaked his hand into hers, comforting her. "Hey," he whispered. "It's going to be great. Just... relax."

She melted at his reassuring smile. "I don't know why I'm so nervous. I mean... it's not like we've never been to something like this before."

"Just remember on the red carpet; step, smile, repeat," he said with a toothy grin.

That part was easy, high heel shoes notwithstanding. "I just hope the ceremony doesn't run too long," she said. "I'm starting to feel the effects of our early morning wake up call."

"It's not like you not to sleep on the plane." Rowan retrieved the invitation from his jacket pocket as the car pulled up in front of *Le Louvre*.

"Is there such a thing as being too tired to sleep?" she asked as the attendant opened the door and Rowan climbed out, turning back to take her hand.

Step. Smile. Repeat. Don't fall down. Lauren's mind was on autopilot, but a gentle reminder didn't hurt.

AN ATTENDANT at the door took their invitation and inspected it. "*Suis-moi,*" he said, then repeated in English. *Follow me.* Rowan didn't need the translation. He knew the drill. They fell in behind the man as he led them towards the front of the room.

When the escort stopped and pulled out a chair for Lauren, it was at a table that was second from the front, in the middle of the room. She had a great view of the lectern and the two large video screens at the front of the ballroom. A PowerPoint scrolled through the evening's announcements, welcoming everyone to the event and providing information about the agenda and the post-ceremony gala in multiple languages.

Rowan, ever the extrovert, introduced himself to the other guests at their table as they were seated. Lauren smiled and nodded politely as he introduced her. She stopped, recognizing the young woman seated to Rowan's left. "Mia Flückiger," she introduced herself, pushing her glasses up her impish nose. She was the young activist who'd gained notoriety for being vocal and speaking out against the United States environmental policies, or lack thereof. She wasn't even in high school yet, but her use of social media to communicate her ecological concerns had gained quite a global following. Lauren had seen some of her videos on YouTube, and while she did not disagree with her; she didn't care overly much for the delivery. The child — hardly more than a teen — was haughty to the point of being arrogant. She never hesitated to engage in personal attacks on Twitter when she didn't agree with a politician or a world governmental policy.

"You're the Bigfoot woman," the girl said with disdain when Lauren offered her a hand that went unaccepted.

"You're the environmental activist," Lauren retorted, sitting back in her chair.

"Yes, but global warming is real," she said in her arrogant Swiss accent. "The impact it is having on the world is catastrophic."

"And you're certain of that?" Lauren couldn't help herself.

The girl's face dropped, and her expression turned even more sour. "It is the only thing I am certain of. Our world is being destroyed, and we are the ones doing it."

"And the Bigfoot population is suffering from it as well," Lauren said. "Surely we can agree... we have to do everything we can to stop it."

The girl just looked at her flatly, twitching her nose, then turned her attention to the front of the room as the presenter came to the stage. Lauren pursed her lips and gave Rowan a half-hearted grimace, shrugging.

She breathed a sigh of relief as she caught sight of Bahati and Jean-René as they made their way to the table and took the seats beside her. Bahati reached over and hugged her. "So sorry we're late," she said. "Our flight was delayed."

"At least you didn't need two hours in the salon to get your hair tied up in a fancy ponytail." Lauren smirked.

"But it's a lovely ponytail." Jean-René leaned over Bahati and grinned. "How many trophies do you think we'll go home with tonight?"

Lauren glanced at the girl, who scowled over her shoulder at her. "Maybe none," Lauren said. Combined they were nominated for five awards total. It wasn't just her, two of *The Veritas Codex* episodes had been given nods for various categories including archaeology for their finds in the Yucatán, and another for their episode filmed at NASA covering the new telescope that had been launched. "But it's just an honor to be nominated."

"Screw that," Jean-René scoffed under his breath. "I want to win."

JACOB WAS SITTING in his office, going over the production schedule when the phone rang. He sat up and hit the button on the speaker phone.

"I'm sorry to bother you, sir, but I have a gentleman on the phone from Germany. He says he's trying to reach Dr. Grayson and Mr. Pierce," his assistant said.

"I'll take it," Jacob said. The phone bleeped. Jacob introduced himself, then said, "I'm sorry to have to inform you, but

Dr. Grayson and Mr. Pierce are out of the country on assignment."

The man began a long dialogue in German, and he seemed desperate and excited. Jacob caught something about *Großer Fuß*... "Bigfoot?"

"*Ja*," the man said, pausing.

"One minute," Jacob said, hitting a button the phone. "Selena, do we have someone who speaks German?"

"I took a couple of years of German in high school," she said. "I might be out of practice, but I'm happy to try."

It was a painfully tedious process, but Selena did a good job. The story that unfolded was one Jacob could hardly believe. From the moment his attention was piqued, he began jotting down notes, scribbling just to keep up with the tale. "So the long and short of it is, the detective here wants to know if Dr. Grayson and Mr. Pierce can come and figure this all out before anyone else gets killed by Bigfoot." Selena summarized the detective's request.

"Tell him... I'll do what I can."

"AND THE WINNER of the *Society of Modern Science's Scientist of the Year*, for contributions made to the fields of Archaeology and Anthropology is..." the presenter said, taking the envelop from the stage assistant. He hesitated, adjusting his glasses, peering down at the paper. He cleared his throat overtly and muttered. "This is unlikely," he said. "It... it appears... we have two winners?" A singular gasp arose from the audience as the presenter looked for someone to provide him direction. "Is this right?"

Lauren's brow clamped down over her nose, and her eye met the young ecologist's who gave her an expression of assuredness, as if the award were already hers. The whole thing was an annoying farce; a melodramatic roadblock to her going back to the hotel and getting out of this blasted corset and high heels.

The announcer got the signal to continue and took a deep breath to compose himself. "And the winner is... the *winners are*... Dr. Lauren Grayson & Rowan Pierce, hosts of the television program *The Veritas Codex.*"

Jean-René leapt out of his chair letting out a whoop that cut through the din of polite applause. Lauren sat in stunned silence, her eye going from the angry gaze of the girl to Rowan's right. Truthfully, she hadn't expected to win anything, and certainly not the prestigious *Scientist of the Year* award. Rowan stood with his hand out to his wife. She didn't move. "Lauren," Bahati nudged. "You have to go on stage."

Lauren looked to her friends as Jean-René pulled her chair out, with her still in it. Rowan caught her elbow and helped her up. "Come on, honey," he said.

"We... we won?" She looked at him blankly.

"Of course we won," he said. "We found the lost Maya calendar, not to mention the cenote full of gold and other treasures. We saved the Grolier Codex... and don't forget we caught a diamond thief in Washington State."

Lauren was on the stage before she realized what was happening.

Someone handed Rowan the gold statuette of a woman holding up an oversized atom. He glanced at it as he stepped up to the podium, keeping his hand on Lauren's elbow in case she panicked and tried to run; or passed out. "There are three stages in scientific discovery," he annunciated carefully as he leaned into the mic. Crowds didn't faze him one bit. "First, people deny that it is true... then they deny that it is important; finally, they credit the wrong person. To have my name mentioned here is clearly an error on *someone's* part." The audience laughed. "I just handle logistics. The real science is done not by me, but by my brilliant wife... all the credit goes to her." He turned to Lauren and leaned in. He kissed her quickly. "This one is for you, honey." He shoved the golden statuette into her shaking hands.

Lauren looked at him blankly and realized her knees were trembling. A huge tear welled up in the corner of her right eye and spilled out over her cheek unbidden. She glanced down at the award and then lifted her lashes to peer under them at the crowd. The room spun, and she forced herself to focus on Bahati, who grinned. "A wise old shaman once told me a lesson that has stayed with me... and will stay with me forever. It is a lesson I think we must all learn. He said, *stay curious, always.*"

The rest of the night was a blur. Lauren was leaning heavily on Rowan's arm, her heels in her hands, when they returned to the hotel. Bahati and Jean-René joined them in the Presidential Suite for a late night cocktail. Lauren went to the other room to change and returned in the complementary bathrobe provided by the hotel. She curled up on one end of the sofa in the living room as Rowan stretched out in the Queen Anne-style chair beside her, his tie undone; his shirt sleeves rolled up; a whisky in his hand. Three golden trophies sat on the coffee table in front of her. One was hers and Rowan's, one was for *Best Documentary* for their show on the Maya, and the third was all Jean-René's for *Best Cinematography for a Documentary.* She smiled at it as she yawned, resting her weary head on her fist; her elbow on the arm of the sofa.

"Your trophy case must be getting full," Bahati said, kicking off her shoes. Jean-René handed her a brandy.

"We'll just have to get a bigger one." Rowan picked up one of the golden statuettes, inspecting it. The heft of it was impressive. "Won't we, Lauren?"

"Huh?" She sat up, realizing she'd nodded off.

"Is that your phone?" Jean-René looked puzzled, and Lauren realized she could hear the buzzing too.

Rowan reached over and picked up Lauren's handbag. He took out her phone. "It's Jacob ... bet he's calling to congratulate us." He punched the button and put it on speaker.

"Hi Jacob," Lauren said. "What's up?" It wasn't like him to call, much less to call so late. There was a significant time difference though.

"Whatever you have planned for the next week, cancel it," Jacob said without preamble.

Rowan's brow knitted as his smile faded. The tone in Jacob's voice was disconcerting to Lauren, too. "What's wrong?"

"I've just gotten off the phone with a detective in Germany," he said. "The authorities need your unique... perspective on a case."

"I'm not following you." Lauren sat up, now wide awake.

Jacob related the details of the case. A priest had been murdered, a child attacked, both appeared to have been mauled by a horrible monster. "I'm texting you a picture," he said. "I just got this."

Rowan flicked the phone screen and pulled up the text message as it came in. He took it and held it where everyone could see it as they gathered around.

"*Was ist das?*" Jean-René gasped.

"Is that... a footprint?"

Lauren snatched the phone and zoomed in. "We've seen prints like this before," she said, handing it back to Rowan.

"Is this a... a Bigfoot print?"

"Sure looks like it," Rowan confirmed.

"I'll send you the details," he said. "The police are willing to release the case file for production purposes in exchange for your assistance in solving the case."

"But... we're supposed to be at Rowan's parents' house in Denver for Christmas," Lauren protested. "It's Henry's first."

"I realize it's asking a lot," Jacob said. "But there are concerns that the attacks will continue until this thing is found and stopped."

"Send me the details and I'll make travel reservations," Rowan said. "Maybe we can figure it out in time to still make it home for Christmas."

∼

THE TRAIN from Paris to Frankfurt had taken a few hours, but the drive to Herrenberg was just as long. It was late afternoon when they walked into the police station to meet the detective.

"Dr. Grayson, *mein gute Frau.*" He greeted her. "I'm grateful to you for coming." His English was good, but his accent thick. "I am Detective Schulz. *Herr* Pierce." He offered a hand to Rowan.

Rowan greeted him and introduced the rest of the team. Jean-René had his camera shouldered. He glanced out as the cinematographer was introduced and raised a hand before disappearing behind the viewfinder. "We understand there've been some unusual attacks."

"Please, come." He guided them from the lobby upstairs to an office where he had all the case files and pictures that he pulled up on a screen. "A few nights ago, there was a small child in a rural town in the *Schwarzwald* who was attacked while bringing in the livestock ahead of a storm. It would have been written off as a wolf or a bear, but the child's father found tracks in the mud and snow." He showed them the same picture Jacob had sent.

Lauren's curiosity was already piqued, but the rest of the images she hadn't seen made her heart skip a beat.

"Fearing for the child's life, they called the doctor, as well as the parish priest, who had to travel through the blackwood in the storm." The detective painted a terrifying picture as he told the events as they'd been able to recreate them based on the evidence. "When he didn't arrive, the men of the village went to find him. But this is what they found..." He pulled up a gruesome picture. The priest had been mauled by something. Lauren's hand went to her shoulder unable to feel the scar on her shoulder where a grizzly had gotten ahold of her. The wounds weren't much different than those Lauren sustained after being attacked in the Alaskan wilderness. The frozen flesh was black and blue around the wound. Deep gouges marred the dead flesh of the man's face and chest.

"*Mein Gott*," Lauren gasped, wavering in her chair. Rowan's hand went to hers, fortifying her. "What could do something like that?"

"This is why we called you," Detective Schultz said, clicking the image to the scene. The bloodied snow was riddled with deep tracks that matched the image the farmer had taken. It matched — or was at least similar to—tracks Lauren and Rowan had cast all over the world, but more notably in the Pacific Northwest; and Nepal. "This is something you have experience with, *ja*?"

"Oh, *ja*," Rowan muttered. "Looks like Bigfoot prints."

"The real problem I have with all this," Lauren said, now recovered from the initial shock. "Bigfoot isn't known to maul people... and it looks like whatever attacked the priest used claws... sharp ones."

"Did anyone see it?" Bahati asked.

"What do you know of our traditions in *Schwarzwald*?" the detective asked.

"Isn't this where legends of Saint Nicholas originated?" Rowan asked.

"Among other traditions," he said. "But the blackwood is a superstitious place. The people here are not well-educated. Many of the elderly have never used the internet or a cell phone. The younger citizens have at least been introduced to the modern comforts and luxuries technology provides. Still, the ancient legends are pervasive and well-believed."

"Are there stories of evil spirits in the woods? Malicious pixies? Fairies? Dwarves?" Lauren asked, jotting notes in her journal. "Werewolves?" Her brow arched inquisitively.

"There is a dark minion who is said to serve Saint Nicholas, to ensure those who are on the naughty list are punished. Have you ever heard of Krampus?" His voice had a dark tone that made Lauren look up.

"I have. Krampus is a monster... like Freddy Krueger meets Bigfoot?" Jean-René quipped from behind the camera.

The detective looked at him sternly. "Interesting description... but accurate."

THE TEAM SAT in the dining room of their inn, pints of ale on the hardwood table in front of them, and the perfume of frying potatoes, sauerkraut and schnitzel filled the air. Lauren's stomach growled. As they waited for their meal, Rowan had his iPad out and was searching the web for more information on the horned anthropomorphic monster of Christmas. Lauren made notes in her journal as he related the important details.

"He's called the *Christmas Devil*, or a *Christmas Demon*," Rowan said. "He torments naughty children for their misbehavior."

"Torments or tortures?" Jean-René scoffed, tipping back

his stein. He drained the ale before lifting a finger to the waitress who brought him a second one.

Rowan turned the image on the screen to his wife. "Who does that look like to you?"

"*Baphomet,*" Lauren said. "From occult traditions. Or maybe *Lucifer* himself from the Abrahamic religions."

"It says here, Krampus is an ally of Santa Claus... or perhaps an anti-Santa Claus. He brings suffering and torture to naughty children, whereas Father Christmas brings gifts. Most versions depict it as a malevolent character who would severely beat children into obedience, though in some legends he might outright kill the child."

"I seem to recall something about Krampus putting a child into a sack and beating them with a stick before taking them back to his lair to devour them," Bahati said.

"This site says that its tradition for parents to put out offerings of schnapps to keep Krampus from taking their children, or in payment for the archfiend's efforts to discipline their unruly child."

"Peach or peppermint?" Rowan retorted.

"Does it matter?" Lauren snapped.

Rowan turned back to the iPad. "The name Krampus comes from the Old German *krampen,* meaning..."

"*The claw,*" Lauren said, before he could finish.

"Well, that does match the wounds on the priest's body," Bahati thought aloud.

"You are here for the *Krampuslauf?*" A man approached their table, putting a hand on the back of first Rowan's chair, then Lauren's. He leaned over and introduced himself, in English. "Forgive me for eavesdropping."

"I'm sorry? What's that?" Rowan asked, gazing up over his shoulder.

"The Krampus Run," he said.

"What's a Krampus run?" Bahati asked.

"It's like a Christmas parade," he said. "Except many of us dress up as the Christmas Devil and see how many children we can make scream. I made twenty-six cry last year." He seemed pretty proud of the tormentors.

"Why is that even a thing?" Bahati recoiled. "Why would anyone *want* to make a child cry?"

"We are trying to help make sure they end up on Saint Nicholas' list," he said. "Do you have children?"

"Not yet," Bahati said.

"When your kids are running around acting like fools, you will be glad for someone like me to help them behave."

"Not hardly," Bahati muttered under her breath.

"Come to the *Krampuslauf*," he said. "You'll see. It's very effective."

"We're actually here on business." Lauren spoke in German. "When is this Krampus run?"

"Tomorrow night," he said, clearly impressed with her ability to speak his language. "I will be the most terrifying Krampus there. I will find you and I will make your friend cry." He nodded towards Bahati.

"I don't recommend that," Lauren said.

"How far is it to the village?" Lauren asked from the back seat as the detective pulled out onto the highway.

"In good weather, it's about an hour," he said. "Recent snows have made it a bit more treacherous. The roads are narrow and ill-kept, especially when we get into the mountains."

"Surely it's not as bad as the roads in Columbia," Bahati said.

"Or Peru," Lauren added.

"You're forgetting that road in Nepal," Jean-René said.

"Don't remind me about Nepal." Rowan winced.

"Please reserve your judgment for when we reach the town," the detective said.

Lauren sat back in her seat and caught Bahati's nervous expression. She reached over and caught her hand, finding it icy cold. "Could you turn up the heat, just a little?" Lauren asked in German.

She watched Rowan as the car moved from the city to the rural country-side, then into the mountains. As the hour passed, the fatigue of travel became apparent as his blinking increased, and his lids began to take moment longer to lift. Before long, he was nodding and his chin came to rest on his chest, his arms crossed over his body. Lauren felt it, too. The few hours of sleep on the train the night before, combined with the long travel days that preceded it, they were all exhausted.

Bahati and Jean-René had come to Paris from San Diego, and they weren't in any better shape. Soon, Lauren was the only one of the passengers still awake, even when the car turned off the main road. The car continued, winding through the narrow, paved, single-lane roadways that reminded her of the roadways outside Tahlequah, where she'd been raised. She learned to drive on asphalt roads that hadn't been repaved in decades; where the potholes were bigger than craters on the moon.

When the road seemed to drop out from under them, Lauren was glad she was awake. The paved road gave way to a slushy, sloppy, dirty — muddy — trail. The car fishtailed and everyone was jostled and suddenly wide awake. The noise that erupted from Rowan's throat made Lauren snicker to herself, and she barely had a chance to get control of her face before he turned and looked at her, startled.

"Sorry about that," Detective Schultz said, sheepishly. "This is where we found Father Bernard's car." He pointed to an area where the road was wide. "If he'd gone a few more feet in that drift, he'd have gone over the ledge there."

"So he walked from here?" Lauren asked as they came around the curve and the trees grew even more dense. The gray skies became completely obscured. Snow drifted around the bases of the towering pines. The car hit a pothole and fishtailed in the slush and the back tire spun out, losing all traction.

"I can see why he walked," Jean-René said.

The detective pulled the car over and put it in park. "I'll take you to where it happened," he said. "Bundle up. It's still rather cold here."

He was not wrong.

Lauren was glad they'd been shopping the day before. Having just come from Cambodia, she had shorts and hiking boots and even a bathing suit, but no cold-weather gear. Bahati had at least brought a coat and a couple of sweatshirts. Instead of shopping for Parisian fashions, they'd ended up at *Au Vieux Campeur* buying coats, sweaters, woolen socks, gloves, and hats; practically everything they had on at the moment. Lauren's *toque* was gray and had a soft interior, a fake-fur trim and pompom on top. The flaps came down and covered her ears, with braided yarn ties that she let hang down alongside her braids. Her winter boots kept her feet warm and dry, despite the mud and slushy snow.

Her breath hung in the air around her face as they trod through the dense woods. Rowan reached back and offered a hand as they came to an embankment. He helped Bahati, then took the camera from Jean-René so he could get down as well. Finally, they made it to the clearing.

The snow was still stained with the priest's blood, and footprints of all shapes and sizes cut through the melting snow and mud. Vermin and other scavengers had come looking for a meal. Human tracks suggested the crime scene processors hadn't been discreet, at least not once they had their evidence. At least, that was Lauren's hope. She had no patience for sloppy evidence collection efforts.

Toward the back of the clearing the detective stopped and looked down. "We found many prints like this one, but... the snow makes it difficult to preserve."

Lauren knelt to inspect the large track. This must have been one of the prints they'd seen pictures of. It was massive and looked exactly like the Yeti tracks they'd found in Nepal. "Did you take a cast?"

"A cast?"

"Plaster? Dental stone?" Rowan asked, seeing his wife's expression darken.

"I'll have to check with my team," he said. She suspected they had not.

Lauren stood, her eye going over the detective's shoulder. "Is that the village?" She pointed with her chin.

"It is," he said.

"What happened to the child who was attacked?" Bahati asked.

"He was treated in hospital," the detective said. "His parents are waiting for us."

LAUREN'S HEART broke for the poor distraught mother the moment they were introduced. She was older, the mother of four, according to *Herr Schultz*. The woman, *Frau Baumann*, looked as exhausted as Lauren felt. "Can you tell us what happened?" Lauren asked in German as she sat across from her, leaning in.

"*Es kam ein sturm...*" she began, her voice trembling.

"A storm was coming..." Lauren translated. The woman continued with the tale. "The boy's father had sent him to round up the cattle and bring them into the barn before the blizzard arrived. She couldn't bring herself to imagine what had happened to the boy." She and Lauren carried on a long conversation. The woman fought through her tears to answer the questions the scientist posed. Lauren nodded, putting a hand on the woman's arm, then stood and returned to Rowan and the team who waited nearby.

"He said the monster came after one of the cows, but the herd scattered, and the boy panicked and froze. The monster turned on him when he didn't run," Lauren explained.

"Hm," Rowan thought aloud pinching the tuft of hair beneath his lip as he considered the tale. "Sounds sketchy."

"I think so, too," she said, turning back to the boy's mother. "Can we talk to him?"

The mother looked at her blankly for a moment, and finally acquiesced. "*Ja.*"

LAUREN WENT into the boy's room alone. He was a tiny thing, maybe seven or eight, with dirty blond hair and dull blue eyes. He had a large scratch across his freckled face, and stitches were visible as the furrow disappeared into his hairline. He slipped down beneath the blankets, looking afraid.

"Franz? *Guten morgan*," Lauren said as she came in, then introduced herself. "I'm here to learn more about the monster that attacked you." She sat down on the edge of the bed and tried to imagine what their son, Henry, was going to look like at this age. The boy gazed back at her with cautious reserve. "I've seen monsters before," she said. "So you don't have to worry that I won't believe you."

"You're the Bigfoot lady... from TV," he said in his small voice.

Lauren's brow lifted. "You've seen *The Veritas Codex*?"

"Our teacher at school lets us watch it when we can't go outside for recess," he said.

"Then you know I want to help find the truth," she said. "Can you tell me about what happened, and what you saw?"

The boy nodded. "My father sent me to bring the cattle in, but... I didn't... I was going to, but... I had time... I wanted to play first... I found a cave a few days before and I wanted to go back and leave an apple for the bear that lives there."

Lauren's brow lifted. "A bear?" Bears were extinct in this region; had been since the 19th Century. "Have you seen this bear before?"

"I heard it..." he said. "But... I just saw it in shadows. I have been trying to make friends with it. I take it an apple every time I go that way through the forest. I just found the cave, but... I've been tracking the bear since spring."

"Don't you think a bear would be hibernating this time of year?"

The boy hesitated. "I hadn't thought about that," he said. "I've only read about bears. I've never seen one."

"It's not important." She assured him, but it was. "Okay, tell me what happened."

The boy spun a fantastical tale. He found the bear's cave. The child thought to leave the apple outside, but... curiosity got the better of him, and he dared to venture inside. He thought the apple would be enough of a peace offering to protect him from anything he found in the dark. But instead of finding the beast, he found a treasure trove of items that had been collected and stowed in the cavern.

"What kind of things?" Lauren asked.

"Presents," he said.

"Presents?" Lauren asked. "Just presents?"

The boy just shrugged. Lauren suspected he was withholding information. She gave him the same look her mother had given her when she wasn't telling the whole truth. It was a look that burned through her more than once.

"There were bottles..." he said. "Pretty ones... the kind my mother keeps in the pantry where we can't reach them."

"Alcohol?" Lauren asked.

"My mother and father would never drink alcohol!" He gasped. "Those are... for visitors."

"So, did this *bear* hurt you?" She examined the marks on his face, brushing his hair aside to better see the stitches.

The boy's face tinged red. "No," he said. "When I went to bring the cattle in, something scared them ... I tried to get them to head back to the barn, but they ran the wrong way ... I got knocked down. I think ... They stepped on me ... When I woke up in the field it was snowing. But ..."

"But ..."

"I saw it," he said. "I saw the Christmas Devil." Tears welled up in his eyes.

Lauren considered him for a moment. His eyes shifted nervously, and he looked down at his hands, twisting the blankets in them. "Can you tell me how to find the cave?" Lauren asked.

The boy's eyes lifted to hers. "You're going to find the monster?"

Lauren smiled. "That is what we do."

"Please... don't, *Frau Doktor* Grayson." His dark eyes narrowed as his lips pursed. "I... I don't want you to get hurt."

"I don't want to get hurt, either," she said. "I'll take the police with me."

"But, isn't *Herr* Rowan with you?"

Lauren smiled and nodded. "*Herr* Jean-René and *Frau* Bahati, too."

"They'll protect you... and *Frau* Bahati, too," he said, brightening.

"I'll make a deal with you." Lauren crossed her arms and leaned her elbows on her knees, giving him her brightest smile. "You tell me how to find the cave, and I'll introduce you to Rowan and the team."

His eyes flew open wide. "I can draw you a map!"

"That would be very helpful," Lauren said.

When Lauren came back to join the team, she had a drawing in her hand. Bahati rose, seeing her first. "How is he?"

"Surprisingly good," Lauren said. "He wasn't hurt so badly. Some stitches and scrapes. Probably more frightened than anything."

"He's a good boy," the child's mother said in a thick accent. "But... he doesn't always do what he is told."

"I think this whole rigamarole may change his mind," Lauren said to the woman in German. "He's faced a monster and he's afraid for our team to go back out there."

"You can't be considering it!" The mother gasped.

"That's why we're here," Lauren said, noticing Rowan's concern too. "Franz told me where to find the monster, but he was worried for our safety."

"As he should be," Rowan said. The rest of the company agreed.

"I told him *Herr* Schultz would be with us to keep us safe," she said. "He drew me a map." She held up the page with the crayon drawing on it.

Rowan took it and put it on the table where everyone could study it together. "A cave?" He turned and furrowed his brow as he eyed Lauren.

A dubious expression twisted on her face as she pursed her lips. "I know. Lucky me."

"Caves are rare here in *Schwarzwald*," Schultz said. "The geology doesn't support cave formation."

"Oh?" Bahati asked.

"Caves rarely form in granite or variegated sandstone, which are the predominant geological formation in the region," Schultz said. "Are you certain it's a cave?"

"Yes." Lauren pointed to the drawing. A monster stood at the entrance of a dark void, looking menacing. Line drawings of trees surrounded the cave, along with some rough indication of the mountains and hills along with the field where the stick figure cattle assembled.

Schultz leaned in and studied the map with care. "I think I may know where this cave is."

"You can take us out there in a bit," Lauren said. "I have a promise to keep."

"We're losing daylight," the police officer pointed out.

"This will just take a minute." She curled her finger towards the members of her team. "A little fan wants to meet everyone."

∼

"Two roads diverged in a yellow wood." Jean-René gazed up the dark trail at a fork in the path.

"I think we're lost." Herr Schultz stopped, scratching his head, inspecting the trail where it split. One turned and went down into the valley; the other disappeared up into the deep dark forest.

"No," Rowan said. "We're not lost. Lauren can't get lost."

Lauren had stopped and was gazing up into the tree tops. Rowan knew her well enough to know what she was doing. She listened to the wind in the trees, gaging her place in the universe in relationship to everything else. She was incredibly perceptive when it came to spatial orientation.

"How about you just *blink* us where we need to be," he said, lowering his tone as he leaned into her, putting his finger on his own nose, giving it a wiggle like Samantha on *Bewitched*.

"I wish it were that easy." Lauren turned and looked back behind him. "We've been walking in circles," she said, a little louder for the benefit of the group.

"It's so dark," Bahati said, her breath visible in the dim moonlight. "How long are we going to stay out here?"

Rowan glanced at his watch. It wasn't all that late, but he understood now why it was called the Black Forest. A snowflake spiraled down between the branches and was soon joined by more.

"We should head back," Lauren said apprehensively. "A storm is coming."

"Of course it is." Jean-René bristled, flicking off his camera.

"Think we can make it back to town before the *Krampuslauf*?" Rowan asked.

"Just be sure you pick up a couple of bottles of schnapps," Schultz said. "You can't face down the Christmas Devil empty-handed."

"I'm going to need a couple of shots myself, if you want me to go to the Krampuslauf," Bahati said, looking dubious.

"Don't worry, *ma petite*," Jean-René said, putting an arm around her. "I will protect you from the demons."

"But who's going to protect me from you?"

With a belly full of good German food and a tankard of beer, Rowan was a much happier camper. Lauren just picked at her food. She was a million miles away. "If you don't eat all your dinner, Krampus will know. He'll come after you with a switch." Rowan nudged.

"Yeah, sure. That sounds good," Lauren said. She was oblivious to what he'd said.

"And I'm going to paint my butt purple and do the cha-cha to see if Krampus will chase me." Rowan furrowed his brow at Jean-René and Bahati.

"You too?" Bahati said with a bemused grin. "I was thinking neon green, but purple works."

"I like purple." Lauren sniffed and stabbed a bite of potato, snatching it off the fork with her teeth, still oblivious to their teasing, or the reason for it. She looked up at Bahati. "Green isn't your color."

"Yellow?"

A shoulder lifted. "Maybe," Lauren said.

"What is up with you?" Rowan nudged her.

She looked at him blankly. "What?"

"It's like you're a million miles away."

"Just thinking," she said flatly.

"About?"

"Bigfoot," she said.

Rowan's brow lifted. "Bigfoot?"

"I thought we were investigating Krampus?"

"What if Krampus is just the local version of Bigfoot?" Lauren asked. "Species diversity would account for the differences in the descriptions between Bigfoot. The same goes for Yeti, Yowie, Yerin, all the various adaptations of the creature."

"You're forgetting one thing," Bahati said. "While Bigfoot throws rocks and scares hikers in the woods, Krampus beats small children and takes their Christmas presents."

"Besides, he's supposed to be half-goat, half-demon," Jean-René added.

"The anthropomorphic variations are easily explained," Lauren said. "People, especially children, make horrible witnesses. Doubly so when they're afraid. Maybe... they all got it wrong."

"I could see that," Rowan said. "But..." he leaned in and lowered his tone. "Don't you have some *connection* to... you know... Bigfoot?"

"Just the one," Lauren said softly. "Still, I can't help but wonder."

"Well, after all that food, I'm ready to go see what this *Krampuslauf* is all about," Rowan said. "Maybe walk off this food baby."

LAUREN STOPPED as they reached the center of town, surprised by the sheer number of people crowding the sidewalks of the narrow streets. The atmosphere felt festive, as most holiday parades did. Swags of greenery and white twinkling lights draped across the road and wreaths were hung on the doors of the ancient buildings.

Patient children sat on the curbs, awaiting the start of the festivities. They knew better than to misbehave with so many

Christmas Devils coming out soon. A few looked nervous, as if they knew the Devils were coming just for them. Perhaps they had good reason. "Where's the best place to set up?" Jean-René carried the camera and tripod on his shoulder.

A woman with a clipboard came over and looked at them, saying something in German.

"Media, yes," Lauren said, rummaging in her pocket for the small wallet she carried. She produced a business card and explained their purpose. The woman directed the team to a spot and Lauren passed on the information to Jean-René.

He set up and Lauren found the audio equipment in the bag Rowan carried from the hotel. Bahati rummaged through the bag and handed Lauren the mic pack, then stood by as she ran the wire up her sweater, clipping the mic to the collar. Lauren's head lifted up as she was assaulted by a sudden flurry of snow from overhead. Large flakes swirled in the air and landed lightly on her hair and shoulders, as well as those of the team. Normally, she would have been annoyed by such a sudden change in the weather, but tonight, it gave the street of the ancient city a festive glow.

"Sound check. Check. Check."

Bahati gave her the thumbs up as Jean-René finished setting up the camera. Lauren handed Rowan his mic-pack and he did the same. "Okay," he said, turning to Lauren. "I'll give the audience just a bit of history on Krampus and the *Krampuslauf*. Then, you can talk about the attack on the priest and the child and how we got called off of another project to come and investigate."

"That'll do," she said.

Drums echoed on the buildings, accompanied by what sounded like tinkling bells — not jingle bells though — more like rattling chains. In the distance, beyond where they could see, the rise of screams from the children at the beginning of the parade route pierced the din of the waiting crowd, and the gasps of those around them rose. There was an initial panic as a couple of the children jumped to their feet and backed into their parents, seeking protection from the coming monsters.

"We better roll." Lauren turned back to the camera. "Everyone ready?"

She glanced at each of them. Jean-René gave her a thumbs up. Bahati nodded. Rowan said, "Let's do it."

"And we're on in 5... 4... 3... 2..." Jean-René counted it down and pointed at Rowan as the light on the top of the camera went red.

"Every year in early December, children in Germany and Central Europe begin to prepare for the arrival of St. Nicholas. They know, if they've been good, he will reward them with presents and sweets. But not every child is promised such joy. Children who have been naughty will find a lump of coal, in place of presents. Worse, they will have to face the Christmas Demon — Krampus," Rowan spoke confidently into the camera, his thumbs hooked into the pockets of his winter vest as he leaned in and raised his voice over the hum around them. The drumbeats increased in tempo and volume as he spoke. "Who is Krampus you ask? He is the half-man, half-goat who comes every year to chase naughty children, stuff them in a bag, and beat them with a stick. The legend comes from a pagan tradition and later became part of the Christian traditions in which St. Nicholas visited children to reward them around the 5th or 6th of December. Around this time, his menacing counterpart makes his visit as well. This is known as *Krampusnacht*, or Krampus Night. Tonight, we're in southern Germany where the tradition takes on another interesting term. Tonight, we're guests at the annual *Krampuslauf*, or the Krampus Run."

Lauren watched him as he spoke and sensed when he was

done with his introduction. "But tonight, *The Veritas Codex* team is here for more than just tricks and treats. We've been called away from a previous assignment at the request of the local police to help solve a recent mystery, the murder of a priest, and the attack on a small child. And all the evidence points to a singular suspect, none other than the Christmas Demon himself... Krampus."

Screams rose wildly behind her as the parade of demons reached their block and children, and adults alike, panicked and ran to escape the costumed monsters who walked down the middle of the snow-covered lane. Lauren turned as Jean-René panned over her shoulder. A cart with a wicked monster in a metal cage was pulled down the street by volunteers in their best winter apparel. Men in fur-covered suits, adorned with horrific masks with twisted visages and horned crowns, growled and roared at the children. Each one was more horrific than the last. Some were dark and very much satanic looking while others looked like fur-covered gargoyles with wings that spread to impressive wingspans. Meanwhile, others looked like the dark hairy beast the *Veritas Codex* crew was more accustomed to, though most were horned with fangs and great claws.

About the time Lauren was ready to turn back to the camera and continue her narration, one monster broke from the crowd and came running directly towards Bahati whose back was turned to the street. She held the parabolic dish; adjusting audio to filter out some of the background noises.

The beast grabbed her around the waist and tossed her over its shoulder, ripping the headphones off her head. Lauren caught the dish as the demon absconded with Bahati. Rowan turned back to Jean-René. "Are you going to let the monster steal your wife?"

"Pshaw," the cameraman scoffed, waving off his boss. "Let the beast have its fun."

"Are you serious?"

"That's the dude from dinner the other night," he scoffed. "My she-beast won't hurt him... much."

Rowan and Lauren shared a surprised but bemused glance between them, just as another beast ran towards them roaring. Lauren nonchalantly held up a hand and cocked a hip to one side. "Please," she said with derision. "I'm on St. Nicholas' *nice list*," she added. "You have no power here."

The monster hung its head and arms dejectedly. Then lifted his mask. "Where's your little friend, I know I can make her scream." It was the man from the hotel restaurant. Lauren did a double-take.

"Wait..." Jean-René froze, a horrified look on his face. "That wasn't you that absconded with my wife?"

"I promised her I could make her scream," he said. "Did someone beat me to it?"

A stunned expression overtook the camera man's face and his color drained as he stood, slack-jawed; stunned. A split second later, he ripped off his headphones, abandoned his camera and raced off into the snow to rescue his wife.

"Good morning," Rowan said as he held the chair out for Lauren. There was a palpable discord between Bahati and Jean-René. Clearly, she was still angry. "How'd you sleep?"

His chipper attempt at levity didn't work. "On the floor," Jean-René grunted.

"Oh," Rowan said, gulping. "Sorry."

The waiter arrived and filled Lauren's cup, then filled Rowan's.

"Are we going back to the forest today?" Jean-René asked.

"Probably not," Lauren said. "I thought we might go to church instead."

"Church?" Rowan furrowed his brow. "I've never known you to be... religious."

"I may not be religious, but I am... spiritual," she said. "Besides, where else would we go to interview people who knew the priest?"

"Silly me," Rowan said. "Should have known."

"Count me in," Jean-René said. "Perhaps I can get in a quick confession before my wife sends me to meet my maker." He kept his head down and good thing. Bahati's eyes lifted for the first time and the expression could have burned through her husband's soul.

THE CHURCH BELLS rang out across the valley as others assembled and entered as well. Lauren was not well-versed in the subtle nuances of the Catholic faith, though she had studied the dogma. Bahati had gone through catechism before she and Jean-René had married. He was a devout Catholic, even if he didn't make it to Mass as often as most.

Lauren watched Jean-René and Bahati and modeled their behavior as they found an empty row near the back of the chapel. She didn't miss the cautious gazes cast in their direction by the suspicious natives who'd never seen these outsiders before.

Even when the service ended, the less-than-welcoming stares fell on them as others rose and made their way out of the church. Before the *Veritas Codex* team could make their way out, the priest came around behind them and made an overt noise, as if clearing his throat. "*Willkommen. Gott sei mit dir.*" *Welcome. God be with you.*

"And also with you," Lauren answered back, recognizing the common recitation that had been part of the earlier service.

"I'm Father Acwulf," he said, in heavily German-accented English. "Are you visiting our parish from the States?"

"We're investigating your predecessor's death," Rowan said, keeping his tone low as the last few parishioners exited. The team followed.

He nodded, sensing the need for discretion. He took Rowan's arm and led them over to a quiet alcove, away from the exit. "The ladies of the church typically make luncheon for the staff. Will you join me in the rectory?"

"We've recently eaten," Lauren said, not the least bit hungry after the morning's feast. "But we'd be happy to keep you company."

The priest seemed pleased by that. "Come," he said.

"FATHER JOHAN HAD a bit of a reputation, you see," Acwulf said as he sliced into the sauerbraten and potatoes on his plate. A bottle of wine had been opened and offered to the guests but had been declined. "We each have our vices, but Johan seemed to have them in spades. I often took his confession myself when I came to visit."

"I thought the confessional was... protected," Lauren seemed taken aback by the priest's candor. She suspected he would tell them each of his vices, if given the chance.

"His faults were well known to all," Acwulf said. "But, it is not my place to justify or qualify the man's sins," the priest said, wiping his mouth on the napkin. "He is with God now. He will be judged by the Almighty."

"How long had Father Johan served this parish?" Lauren asked.

"Nearly twenty years," Acwulf said, taking a bite and chewing thoughtfully. "He may have had his flaws, but he was well-loved by the community he served. He did many good deeds to help these people. They feel his loss profoundly."

"And will you be taking over in his wake?" Rowan asked.

"My superiors asked me to fill in until a decision can be made," he answered. "I have my own parish and assist with several others. I am only here a few days a week."

"And what do you know of the boy who was attacked? Of his family?" Lauren sat back, jotting notes in her journal.

"The father is hardworking. He's a mechanic. I've had him work on my car before. He charges a fair price and does quality work. The mother runs the nursery at the church on Sundays and works part-time at the bakery. I've only met her once, but she seems kind. Her children seem well-behaved, but the little one, Franz? He is a ... a challenge. *Frau Bienbrik* says he's always in trouble at school. She mentioned he tells big stories so grandiose they can't possibly be true."

"Surely you told a few tall tales when you were that age?" Rowan quipped.

"The Lord detests lying but delights in people who are trustworthy." The priest looked affronted. "Bearing false witness is as harmful to oneself as it is to others. In the book of Proverbs, it says there are seven things the Lord hates: haughtiness, lying, murdering, plotting evil, eagerness to do wrong, false witness and sowing discord among brothers. It also says a false witness shall be punished."

Lauren looked at Rowan, contorting her lips in silent frustration. She turned to the priest. "Thank you for your hospitality, but I fear we've taken enough of your time." She stood, and the rest of their party followed suit.

"At least stay for dessert, Frau Grayson," Acwulf looked up at her almost wounded. "You've heard of our famous Black Forest Cake? *Ja*? *Frauline Bienbrik* makes the best cake in the region. Surely you can't say no to a slice of her cake."

"Actually, we can," Lauren said apologetically. "Please, take no offense."

"None taken." He rose, laying his napkin on the chair as he vacated it. "It has been my pleasure." He bowed. "Go with God."

～

"WELL, THAT WAS A WASTE OF TIME." Lauren sighed as they stood at the car, debating what to do next. The snow had stopped but mounded in drifts around the edge of the parking lot that had been cleared by plow that morning. The roads had cleared, but the grassy surfaces were completely covered.

"Maybe," Rowan said, about to say something else when Lauren's phone rang in her pocket. She held up a finger and fished it out.

"It's Schultz," she said.

"Dr. Pierce," he said, without preamble. "There's been another attack. Where are you?"

～

LAUREN KNELT at the edge of the road, inspecting the corpse. She was grateful for the cold temperatures. The odor would have been much worse in the summer. The bovine victim had been ripped to shreds, chunk of flesh had been devoured and entrails had been ripped from the abdominal cavity and gnawed on.

"Well, we can eliminate at least one suspect," Rowan stood with his jacket pulled over his nose. He turned to the camera. "It wasn't *El Chupacabra*."

"The goat sucker?" Schultz asked.

"*Chupacabra* just leaves a puncture wound." Bahati nodded.

"You've seen a *Chupacabra*?"

"We found some compelling evidence," Jean-René said from behind the camera.

"Wild dogs with mange, if you ask me." Bahati sniffed.

"You can't discount the DNA we got off that hair sample though," Rowan pointed out.

Lauren gazed at him dubiously. The sample, collected from a telephone pole, could have come from a boar or a number of other creatures, but all the tests had been inconclusive. Lauren knew as well as Glen at the lab, DNA left exposed to the elements could easily degrade. The sample, upon analysis, appeared quite aged.

"Well," she said, swallowing hard, sniffing into the elbow of her jacket. "Any wild animal will do what it has to in order to feed. Predation is different depending on the species..." She took a step back. "However, the end results are usually the same."

"At least it wasn't a human this time," Bahati said, wincing at the sight. "Do we know who the cow belonged to?"

"That will be difficult to determine," Schultz said. "We have a problem in the Black Forest."

"Oh?" Lauren lifted a brow as she ran her cold hands together and tucked them under her armpits. She'd forgotten her gloves in the car but hadn't wanted to go back for them.

"It is illegal to allow cattle to graze in the blackwood."

Shultz scanned the dense woods just a few yards from the roadway. "This isn't even an indigenous species of cattle. This is a Scottish Highland cow... or it was." He reached for the pack of cigarettes in his shirt pocket but stopped short. "How these beasts get through this dense woods with horns like that, it's a wonder."

"The chamois and elk manage well enough, I suppose," Lauren said, tucking her hands in the pockets of her down coat. "What other animals might do something like that? Are boar common here?"

"Not as much as they used to be," he said. "The livestock allowed to graze in the protected forest are responsible for deforestation. Their impact cannot be understated. Did you know? They account for the loss of nearly one hundred acres a year, on average. They tear up the undergrowth which contributes to run off and mudslides during the rainy seasons. They contribute to the contamination of run off and their wastes cause the nitrogen levels to go up in the surrounding tributaries, which impacts the health of our rivers and streams. The problem is much more widespread than people realize. The governmental agencies assigned with protecting the forests are short-handed, and the police can do little without jurisdiction. We can write warnings and refer to the appropriate authorities."

Lauren pursed her lips as she considered his words. "Predators?"

"Lynx, badgers, foxes, wolves... nothing of considerable size."

"And no bears?"

"The last known Eurasian brown bear was shot and killed in 1835 in the Bavarian Alps," Shultz explained, stepping aside as his forensics expert stepped in to snap pictures.

Lauren gingerly picked her way over the slushy ground

towards the trees. Rowan was on her elbow, a hand ready to help her should she slip. Jean-René had the camera rolling and had since they'd arrived and started their survey of the scene.

"We aren't that far from where we were the other day," Lauren said. She turned to Rowan as she took the child's drawing from her pocket and unfolded it. Studying it moment, she scanned the trees, finding a path she hadn't seen from the road. "Come on," she called back.

"Lauren, wait!" Jean-René called as she sprinted ahead, heedless of any danger.

Rowan was left behind too, startled by her abrupt move. He froze at the cameraman's beckoning, torn between running after her or helping him with the equipment. Logic won the day and Rowan turned to chase after his wife before she magically disappeared, as she was oft to do.

"Lauren!"

BAHATI HELPED her husband with the camera, taking the tripod as he shouldered the rig and took off after the bosses who were well out of sight. Schultz huffed behind them as they raced over rugged terrain. Spots where the snow had melted were muddy, and shaded areas remained slushy. The sodden quagmire delayed them, weighed down with equipment as they were. Lauren, with no such load, had gotten a decent head start, but her muddy tracks provided the team with direction when they came to a fork in the road.

"Lauren!" Bahati called, panting. "Rowan!"

The rustling of dried branches and squishing of boots in the quagmire ahead came to an abrupt halt and Bahati skidded to a stop, losing her footing and landing flat on her butt in a slushy puddle. Lauren stood frozen, with Rowan in front of her, shielding her from the shadowed beast that growled at the entrance of a dark cave.

Jean-René broke through the clearing a moment later, stumbling to avoid stepping on Bahati, but catching his foot on a rock, landing flat on his face, his camera landing lens down with a sickening crack.

Shultz came panting in behind them a moment later. "*Mein Gott!*" He gasped, crossing himself as the beast moved slowly from the shadows and into the dim light of the dense wood. It grunted and snarled, as Rowan backed up, forcing Lauren back a few steps 'til she stood even with Bahati who sat shaking the mud off her hands. Jean-René pushed himself up onto his knees, mud splattered his face, covering the front of his coat and all down the front of his pants. Their Director of Photography reached for the camera, his eyes fixed on the monster moving towards them. Raising the video equipment to his shoulder, he flicked it on, before he realized it was covered in mud. He tried wiping it off with a muddy hand, then realized the futility of it. Tugging out his shirt tail, his eyes shifted from what he was doing to the terror before him.

Bahati scrambled to her feet, mindless of her muddy pants, standing beside Lauren. The two shared cautious gazes. The beast stood head and shoulders taller than Rowan, who looked like a child compared to the beast. Horns protruded from the side of its head, and long fur hung from its muscular body. What appeared to be skulls of small animals had been tied into the matted clumps of hair, along with other trinkets she couldn't identify.

"Easy..." Rowan said softly, trying to soothe the beast as they stared one another down. The beast responded with a deep growl. "We're not here to hurt you..."

The beast snapped at him, and Rowan jumped back, knocking Lauren down, who in turn, knocked Bahati down.

She landed in the same mud puddle she'd just escaped. Lauren glanced back at her then turned to the beast and stepped past Rowan.

"Shame on you! That wasn't nice!" Lauren snapped, challenging the monster. Bahati gasped at the gall. She was stunned when the beast took a step back and dropped its head and shoulders like a scolded dog. "We're not here to hurt you, but that doesn't mean you can snap at us just because you're a big scary monster."

"Lauren?" Rowan drug her name out. Whether it was a warning or a question of her motives, Bahati couldn't be sure. She was even more surprised when the beast took a step back, running its toe in the snow, and lifted its eyes to her cautiously.

It grunted a soft moan of what sounded like an apology as Lauren turned and offered her a hand up. "Lauren, what are you doing?" she asked under her breath.

"Teaching a bully a lesson," she answered softly.

Lauren turned back to the monster. "So." She crossed her arms. "What do you have to say for yourself."

The growl that came from the beast's chest sounded distinctly like '*schlecht*.'

"*Bad*?" Lauren asked. "I'm not bad."

The beast's finger went to its own chest as it looked at her sheepishly. "*Ich war schlecht,*" it said.

"Yes, it would appear you have been bad," Lauren said. "Scaring us like that. It's not very nice."

"Lauren?" This time, Rowan's question was clear.

Bahati took a step up, putting herself at Lauren's elbow. "What are you doing?"

Lauren ignored her question. "So? What do you have to say for yourself?"

"*Es tut mir leid.*" The beast spoke so clear, Bahati could

make out the words, even if she didn't know what they meant. Lauren understood though. *I'm sorry.*

"Well, sorry doesn't begin to make things right," Lauren said. "Did you hurt the farmer's boy?"

"*Es war ein unfall,*" the beast said, backing up.

"An accident, huh?" Lauren said.

The monster explained sheepishly. He had followed the boy who had left an apple in his cave and had intentions of leaving an equal offering for his kindness. He hadn't intended to frighten the cattle, but when they stampeded, he found the boy injured in the field as the snow began to fall.

Lauren translated the story to the rest of the team. "He carried the boy back toward the village and left him where his father would find him. He stayed in the shadows until he was sure the boy was safe." She looked past him, her eye catching something shiny in the cave behind him as a beam of daylight broke through a break in the trees. "Have you... have you been taking things? Things that aren't yours?"

"*Schlecht,*" it repeated. Lauren took a step past him, leaving the rest of the team and the stunned detective speechless and frozen behind her as she peered into the cave, hesitating to enter.

"What's all this?" She stepped into the cave and inspected the treasure-trove. Bahati dared to step past the beast to follow her boss, not wanting her to get too far into the cave without someone to help her. She knew how much Lauren hated small spaces and was surprised to see her enter so brazenly. The cave, however, wasn't that small. It was massive.

Piles of wrapped presents had been stowed in caches, some of which stood shoulder high on Lauren. Rowan appeared at her elbow. Bahati looked at him cautiously. His gaze was locked on Lauren and the scene around her.

"Look," Bahati gasped. "Are those...?"

"Bottles of schnapps?" Rowan asked, stepping up and picking up one of the bottles. "So it would seem."

The beast's cry sounded for a moment like Chewbacca when Han Solo got turned into a block of stone. Lauren turned and scolded it. "We're not going to take your stuff, but... if this is stolen, that police officer over there may have a thing or two to say about all this."

The beast cried again and dropped to its knees, whimpering as if pleading.

"Did you... take all this stuff?" Schultz said, finding his voice.

"...*von den bösen kinder*." The beast sniffed.

"If you took it from the bad children, what did you intend to do with it all?"

"...*für die guten kinder*," it admitted.

"It's for the good children?" Lauren asked.

Bahati walked back over to inspect the beast, who was docile enough. "Excuse me for saying this, but this is the nicest monster I've ever encountered." Shultz translated it for the beast.

"*Nein. Ich war schlecht*," the beast said. *No. I am bad.*

"The priest? Did... did you kill the priest?"

"*Nein. Ich habe nicht getötet. Ich habe versucht zu helfen.*"

Lauren paused in her investigation to return to the mouth of the cave. "You tried to save him?"

"*Von einer wildkatze*," the beast said.

"From a wildcat?" Schultz said.

"Is that even possible?" Lauren asked. Rowan came up behind her. She took a moment to translate the conversation.

"There *are* wildcats in the region." Schultz shrugged.

The beast rose, and everyone drew back in reflex. It paused, shaking its horned head. It held out its arm, pointing to it.

Bahati moved in to inspect the monster's arm. "Are you... hurt?"

"*Von einer wildkatze,*" the beast said. "*Wildkatzen haben auch Rinder getötet.*"

"What'd he say?" Rowan moved in and inspected the wound. It was a long, angry red scratch that was festered and oozing.

"He said a wildcat did it. He says wildcats have been killing cattle too," Lauren translated.

"That looks painful," Rowan said, lifting his eyes to the beast. Bahati came over and pulled a small first aid kit out of her bag. She realized the beast didn't have horns. He had on some kind of hat, like a buffalo head; fur covered and horned. "Can I help?" Rowan asked, drawing Bahati's eyes back to the wound as Rowan set to treating the beast.

"So, let me get this straight," Jean-René finally spoke, the camera useless on his shoulder with the mud caked in the broken lens. "You took those presents from the bad children... to give to the good children? Like Robin Hood?"

Lauren asked the question again for the beast, then turned to Jean-René. "Exactly."

The beast said something else, and Lauren turned to the team. "He was trying to catch the priest to see if he could help him get the toys to children who deserved presents when the wildcat attacked. They got separated, and when he found him, the priest was dead."

"So not only do we have a wild monster running through the wood, but there's also a killer wildcat on the loose?" Rowan furrowed his brow at his wife.

The Krampus looked at Rowan as if he'd understood the comment; he looked wounded at having been called a monster. "Sorry." He went back to tending the injury.

Lauren had a dozen questions for the beast that she asked

while Rowan cleaned the wound, then added some antibiotic ointment, and bandaged the beast's arm. They learned the creature wasn't the Christmas Devil he'd been touted to be and was remorseful for having hurt the boy. He hadn't meant to harm him, but he was afraid the cattle might gore him and was trying to shoo him home. The monster knew this to be one of the children on his naughty list, but he wasn't one to see a child hurt. "The rumors of him whipping children was an exaggeration, blown up more and more over time."

"So, we solved the mystery?" Rowan asked.

Lauren nodded. "I guess we did."

The beast said something else. "Toys?" She turned and looked at the cave. "Yes, I suppose we could find a way to see that they get to the children of the village."

Jean-René stared down his long nose at his boss. "Are you serious?" He laughed curtly. "Really? What happened to the evil monster that chased children and made them scream? What happened to Krampus... the Christmas Devil?"

The beast looked genuinely ruined and said something that made Lauren's jaw drop.

"What?" Bahati asked. "What'd he say?"

"He said his name isn't Krampus," Lauren said. "He's not a Devil."

Lauren spoke to the beast who answered her every question. She looked puzzled by the protracted story the beast seemed to tell. Finally, Bahati leaned in and asked. "What's he saying?"

"He knows the men of the village dress up as him; make fun of him," Lauren explained. "It makes him sad to miss out on the parades and parties. He... he wants to come too."

"He wants to be in the parade?" Rowan furrowed his brow. "But they've already done the parade for the year."

Lauren paused a moment to consider it. "They have for this

year, but... I bet I can get him an invitation to next year's parade." She turned back to the beast and the conversation continued. The beast's eyes seemed to light from within as she laid out her plan.

QUIETLY, Rowan and Lauren arranged to have the cache of toys delivered to the children of the village, with the help of Father Acwulf. Detective Schultz arranged for the truckload of presents to be collected and delivered to the parish.

Once that detail had been tended to, Lauren went in search of the man they'd met at the restaurant at the hotel. It took hours of interviews with the barkeeper, hotel staff, and others to pin down the man's identity.

Lauren found him at the local bakery. He was a pastry chef who sold his products to hotels and cafes in the small village. He seemed surprised when Lauren walked into his shop.

"Herr Babler," she said brightly. "Good to see you again."

"Frau Pierce. Call me Babo," he said. "To what do I owe this honor? You come for the streusel perhaps?" He looked towards the door and out the shop window. "Where's your little friend? I never found her at the *Krampuslauf.*"

"She's making our travel arrangements," Lauren said. "We're headed home tomorrow."

"Did you enjoy the monsters? The parade?"

"We did, very much." Lauren considered him a moment, glancing past him, noticing they were the only two in the shop. If he had any staff, they'd already been sent home for the day. "You guys really know how to throw a party here."

"Old traditions mean we have plenty of time to work out the details," he said, his cheeks lifting into a smile. He hesitated a moment. "Why do I sense you are not here for the strudel, Frau Pierce?"

Her smile cracked and she chuckled. "You are correct," Lauren said. "I have a proposition for you. A friend of mine wants to participate in the Krampus run next year. I thought you might be able to help him out."

He put one hand on his hip and leaned on the counter. "It's a pretty complicated process to get through," he said. "The committee has to approve the costume and judge the potential Krampus before. They must scare an acceptable number of children to be approved."

"Oh, I think my friend will be able to do that," she said.

"Does he have a costume? Every detail must be perfect."

"I think you'll be impressed," Lauren said. "What time does your shop close? I'd like to take you to meet him."

The baker glanced at his watch. "Business is slow." He reached for the strings on his white apron. "Give me a few minutes to clean up and I'll close early." Lauren nodded, smiling as she stood at the counter. "Tell you what, let me get you a pastry and a coffee while you wait."

A smile broke over her face. "I'd like that."

HERR BABLER — Babo — recovered from the initial shock once Lauren had fully explained the situation. He'd been skeptical at first. At long last he agreed to the plot. He wasn't sure how he'd get the rest of the Krampus Association to agree to the scheme, but he assured Lauren he'd help her friend. Assured the Christmas Devil had a friend and ally in the baker, she was able to return to the US with a sense of peace.

Lauren was finally able to get a long and relaxing nap on the flight across the Atlantic. It was Christmas Eve when the plane landed at Denver International Airport. "I feel terrible that I didn't get to do any Christmas shopping." Lauren said as they waited for their bags.

"Same here," Bahati said. "So many cute shops in Germany, but when would we have had time?"

"Don't worry about it," Rowan said, glancing at Jean-René with a gleam in his eye. "We got it covered."

Lauren wrinkled her brow and pursed her lips. "Oh?"

"Henry's going to be so surprised," Rowan said. "Come on." Their bags appeared and they hurried to get them and catch the shuttle to pick up the rental car.

ROWAN'S CHILDHOOD HOME, a two-story rambling ranch-style, had been decorated to the nines. Red and white bulbs outlined the eves, gabled edges, and ridge of the house. A lighted Santa Claus stood by the chimney, waving. A sleigh and eight tiny reindeer in white twinkling lights illuminated the snow on the hipped edge.

Candy-cane lights lined the driveway and sidewalk, which led to the front door. A pine wreath with Stewart plaid ribbon adorned the portal. Rowan didn't need to knock. He threw open the door and shouted, "Merry Christmas!" In his deepest 'Santa' voice.

Lauren had texted his parents, so they didn't seem at all surprised when they arrived. Charles held Henry who was dressed in his footed pajamas. He looked like a little elf, and his face brightened as he saw his parents at the door.

A shriek erupted from his throat as he pushed away his grandfather, climbed over the dog, and got to his feet, toddling towards his mother. Lauren froze, gasping, her hands going to her mouth. "He's walking?"

"He's been cruising around the coffee table all day, but... that's his first steps," Martha Pierce was beaming. Rowan got to Henry before she could. He scooped him up and hugged him, but Henry just wanted Lauren.

"Merry Christmas, Momma," Rowan said, handing him over.

Tears built in Lauren's eyes. Suddenly the long hours of travel no longer mattered. She was home, and she had her baby in her arms... only, he wasn't a baby anymore. She hugged him, then leaned back to inspect him. He grinned brightly. "Merry Christmas, Henry."

"Momma!" Henry beamed.

"Come on," Rowan said. "Time for presents."

"Wait," Martha protested. "It's just Christmas Eve! You have to wait 'til tomorrow for presents."

"Oh come on," Rowan protested. "You always let us open up a present on Christmas Eve." Martha couldn't argue that.

Rowan brought his backpack over to the sofa and sat down as everyone gathered around. Bahati and Lauren sat on each side of him. Henry looked into the bag; wonder written in his eyes. Rowan watched him for a reaction as he pulled out a parcel in brown paper. He couldn't wrap it until he got past airport security, and he'd used a paper bag from one of the fast food restaurants in the terminal.

Henry reached for it. "Mine," he said.

"Can you open it?" Rowan asked.

Henry looked at it, as if trying to solve a puzzle. Rowan found an edge of paper that had torn, and he showed the boy how to pull it. Henry caught on quick and ripped the paper off of the stuffed animal. He lit up as he inspected it, turning it around and over, then froze when he saw what it was; a stuffed Krampus, complete with horns, claws, and bright red eyes.

Henry shrieked and tossed it down on the floor. "No!" He

pointed at the toy, just as Charles' dog snatched it up and ran off to the other room with it. "Bad! Bad toy!"

Rowan laughed. Jean-René nudged him. "Give him the real presents," he urged. "You big meany."

"Well, that's one way to get on the naughty list." Martha scowled at her son.

Rowan reached into the bag. He lifted up the bottle of peach schnapps his friend, Krampus had given him. "It's okay, I've got this."

CHAPTER 2

OF SERPENTS AND SNOW

BY TAMARA GRANTHAM

Animal bones rattled like wind chimes in front of the witch's cabin. I hiked the path to her home, frost-covered leaves crunching under my boots. Spruce trees dusted in snow surrounded me. The air held the fragile scent of autumn fading, of a world transitioning from the warmth of fall to the chill of winter. Ahead, the witch's cabin peeked from the surrounding trees. Snow blanketed the worn logs and sagging roof, camouflaging the structure.

How the place hadn't blown away in one of Encantasia's storms was a mystery.

A brisk wind picked up, tugging my blonde hair across my face and billowing my fur cloak. When I approached the door, dark magic flowed from the cabin. Chills prickled my skin. I grasped the pendant around my neck before walking inside, allowing its magic to warm my hands.

"Get it together, Meara," I whispered to myself. I came here for a reason, and I wouldn't turn around now. Father was barely clinging to life after being attacked by the wyvern only a week before the winter solstice, a time of year when magical creatures possessed the most magic. I'd sworn to do whatever it took to heal him, and I wouldn't be intimidated by a little dark energy coming from a witch's cabin—even if people claimed she killed everyone who trespassed on her land.

Those were nothing but rumors anyway.

"Don't bother knocking," a muffled female voice came from inside. "I hear you. Come in."

Anxiousness quickened my heartbeat at the sound of her voice. My only weapon was a knife I carried in my boot, although I doubted it would be of much use. I had my magic, too, but against a person as powerful as the witch, it would be less useful than the knife.

With a deep breath, I opened the door and stared into the cabin. A fire crackled from the hearth. Other than that, I couldn't make out much more, so I stepped over the threshold and entered the cabin. She hadn't killed me yet. Maybe she was harmless? As my eyes adjusted, I made out the shapes of human skulls sitting on tables.

Maybe not.

I almost turned around and walked straight home, but how could I? No. Father died unless I did this. I stayed. Perhaps those skulls were merely remnants of the wars—ones she'd collected from the battlefield.

With a steadying breath, I searched the cabin. Vials and glass jars lined the cupboards, and books were stacked on every surface. Animal bones littered the floor, and I stepped carefully over them as I approached the woman sitting at the back of the room.

I expected someone with white hair and wrinkled skin, someone wild and half-sane, but this wasn't who I'd envisioned. Her hair fell to her waist in coppery waves. A few tiny braids highlighted the strands, some decorated with beads or feathers. Her dress was a patchwork of gold and crimson fabrics that accentuated her curvaceous frame. The same beads and feathers she wore in her hair also decorated a choker around her neck.

A cat perched on her lap, and she stroked its gray-striped fur without looking up at me.

"You're early," she said.

I tilted my head. "You knew I was coming?"

She heaved a long sigh, then stroked the cat. "She's got much to learn, hasn't she, Ash?" The cat, Ash, I assumed, purred and nudged her hand, then turned its gaze on me. Piercing yellow eyes met mine.

"Tell me your name," the witch demanded.

I gave her a sidelong glance. "You knew I was coming yet you don't know my name?"

She tsked her tongue. "How would I know such a thing? Names are unique to you. No matter of magic or sorcery can reveal a person's name. Only those acquainted most intimately with me know mine, and only a few of them are still alive. Never give your name to just anyone, child. That's lesson one."

"I'm not here for lessons."

"You should be." Finally, she looked at me, and I had to suppress a shudder. Dragon's eyes peered from her face.

I took a stuttered breath. "You're Drau?"

"Was Drau," she corrected. "I haven't lived among the Drau for centuries. I'm no longer one of them. Now, will you tell me your name or not? My patience grows thin. You're lucky I allowed you inside, luckier still to be alive when you did so."

"Got it," I mumbled, then I shook the snow from my cloak and brushed a hand down my leather vest. After traipsing through the forest for half the day, I was sure I had a few briars tangled in my hair. I didn't think a person like the witch would care about my appearance. But being here with her now put me on edge, and I wished I would have at least worn my nice cloak and not the one with patches.

"My name is Meara Wintersong. I'm here to find a cure for—"

"I know why you're here." She waved her hand dismissively.

"—my father," I finished, then placed my hands on my hips. "You knew I was coming, and you know why. What else do you know about me?"

She chuckled, then got to her feet. The cat leapt away and stalked to a corner. "I can discern many things, but not everything."

"How much?" I demanded.

She tapped her lips. "I can't tell you that."

The fact that she knew anything about me was unnerving. I searched the room for crystal balls or scrying screens, but I saw nothing except for her collection of skulls, tatty books, and discarded animal bones. Magic was here, of course. It came to me as a dark presence lurking over my shoulder, almost as a living entity. Yet I knew of no magic that could discover so much about a person. Part of me was curious to learn more about her powers, but my rational side cautioned me to stay away.

The witch paced toward me. She was a head taller than me, which shouldn't have been surprising. She was Drau, after all.

I cleared my throat. "You already know why I'm here, and you haven't killed me yet, so you must be interested in helping me."

"Perhaps so." She circled me. "Perhaps not."

I did my best not to let her intimidate me, so I stood tall and clasped my hands behind my back.

"Meara," she drew out my name. "Daughter of the fallen

king. You're brave to come here. Didn't anyone warn you about me?"

"They did," I answered. "I came anyway."

She arched an eyebrow. "Why?"

"Because I have no cure for wyvern venom. I was told you do."

She laughed softly. "You're unwise to come here when you know so little about me."

I locked my eyes on her. She could be intimidating, but so could I. "It was a risk worth taking. Will you help me or not?"

"If I do, what will you give me in return?"

"I..." I hesitated. What could she possibly want in return? More bones or books, most likely. It seemed those were the only things of value to her.

She walked to me and grasped the pendant around my neck. The marble-sized orb glowed blue against her skin.

"Beautiful," she whispered.

"You can't have it." I snatched it away from her. "I'll die without my magic."

"Ah, yes. The one weakness of the Encantians. You're nothing without your magic, except it's not helping you now." The scorn in her voice taunted me. "Can't save your father, can you?"

"Wyvern magic is too similar to dragon. I can't touch it."

"Then your father should have never confronted a wyvern." She stalked to her chair and sat. "Tell me, how you do you plan to pay me?"

I crossed my arms. She wanted the upper hand, but I'd be a fool to let her have it. "First, if I'm to give you any sort of payment, I need a guarantee that you can help my father. Then, perhaps I'll consider an exchange."

She chuckled under her breath. "You're most certainly Herrald's daughter. Just as headstrong as he ever was."

I tilted my head. "You know his name?"

She gave me a long-suffering look. "Everyone in the four kingdoms knows his name, child."

"True," I conceded, then I sighed. "Am I wasting my time, or will you help me?"

She sat up. A smug glare replaced her smile. "I'll help you, *child*." She repeated the name with disdain. "But since you refuse to tell me what you'll give in return, I shall choose for you." After standing, she crossed to her shelves filled with vials. Glass clinked as she rifled through the jars. She mumbled as she worked, reading labels and tossing empty ones aside.

The cat eyed me from his corner. He sat so still he could have been a statue.

"Ah, here it is." She pulled a vial filled with black liquid from the shelf. Cradling it carefully, she walked to me. "This is the last of it. Once this is gone, I'll have no more."

"What is it?" I asked, eyeing the glass.

"A potion made from the scale of a winter serpent. This is a powerful draught. It could destroy the unwary, and it must be handled with caution."

"Will it cure Father?"

"Yes," she answered. "If it doesn't kill him first."

I crossed my arms. "That doesn't sound reassuring."

Her eyebrows arched. "Yet this is the only potion capable of counteracting wyvern venom."

The vial glittered in her palm, tempting me. "What do you want in return?"

She sucked in a breath. "If I give you this, I will have nothing left from the last scale I collected, so I will need to replenish my store. I want an ice serpent's scale in return."

I frowned. She couldn't be serious. "Impossible. It would take a month to travel to the Ice Realm. Father would be dead by then."

"Not so," she countered, arching an eyebrow. "Not if I were to help you."

"Help me how?" I questioned, not sure I would like the answer.

"I can create a portal to send you to the Ice Realm."

"Really?" I asked, suspicion in my voice. "A portal?"

"Of sorts." She still held the vial in front of her, as if to tempt me.

I weighed my options. I'd never been to the Ice Realm. In truth, I wasn't even sure it existed. It was a place I only read about in my fairy tale books as a child. There were no towns or outposts, and most creatures who inhabited the place were deadly and untamed. Thankfully, there weren't any dragons, but the ice serpent was close enough. I would be lucky to survive an encounter with it, which is why I presumed the witch wanted me to confront it, and not her.

She lost nothing in this deal. If I died, she kept her vial. If I survived and brought back the scale, she could make more potion with it. She had everything to gain, and I had everything to lose. But this was Father's life on the line. I had no other options, and I knew he would do the same for me.

Closing my eyes, I took a deep breath and made my decision.

"All right," I said. "I'll do it. I'll get the scale."

When I opened my eyes, she was smiling, although her dragon eyes glittered with greed. "Good," was her only reply.

She tucked the vial in a pocket, then patted it, as if to tell me *this is still mine*. Then, she turned to her bookshelf and pulled out an old tome. Cracks and tears riddled the leather cover. As she placed it on a table, she stirred a cloud of dust. The book creaked as she opened it.

When she started turning the pages, the cat perked up. He stood and stretched, then strode to the table and perched on top. He sniffed the book, then casually placed a paw on the page she was reading. The witch shooed him. "This is not for you to sleep on." She flipped another page. "Cats," she mumbled.

Ash ambled to me, and I reached for him. He took a step away, sniffed my hand, then sat and stared at me, his tail twitching.

"Good kitty," I said softly, reaching for him again, and he allowed me to stroke his head. As I touched him, my magic emanated. It flowed like tendrils into the cat. He didn't seem to notice, and if he did, he didn't react. My magic warmed inside me, then spread into the animal. I gauged the cat's internal organs. A mental picture formed of the blood flowing through the heart. An orb of glowing ember emanated from his chest. I'd seen something like this before in magical creatures, but never in common house pets. What sort of magic did he possess?

I ran my hand toward his stomach and inspected his digestive system, then moved once again to inspect the rest of his organs.

Nothing seemed out of the ordinary, except for a few flea bites, which I soothed with a whisper of my magic.

Ash mewled.

"There," I whispered. "That's better."

"You've got unique magic, young one," the witch said, glancing up briefly from her book. "Not everyone can perceive animals as you can."

I shrugged nonchalantly. "It's like second nature, really. I've never been without it."

"Don't downplay your powers. You must embrace them."

"I do embrace them." I frowned, annoyance clawing at me. Having the witch give me advice was ridiculous. Where had that advice gotten her? She lived as a hermit in the forest, feared by everyone. No family, no friends—at least, none I knew of.

I never wanted to live like her. In fact, I wanted the exact opposite. One day, I would restore our kingdom, rebuild the castle, and live with my family and an abundance of animals surrounding me, *living* animals, and not piles of bones on the floor.

"Here it is," the witch muttered, running her finger down the page. A sketch of a mountain range had been inked onto the yellowed parchment.

"Are those the Ice Mountains?" I asked.

She nodded. "I'm sending you here." She pointed to a black dot near the peak of the highest mountain. "This is the entrance to the cave of the ice serpent. You must enter quickly." She picked at a tattered patch on my cloak. "You're not dressed for this sort of cold, and the cave will be warm. The temperatures in the Ice Realm will kill you if stay out too long. Do you understand?"

I nodded my agreement.

"Good. Once you enter the cave, follow the path until you reach a waterway. The serpent lives near the river's end. After retrieving the scale, you must return to the mouth of the cave quickly. I will place a spell there that will transport you back here to my home."

She made it sound so simple, and she'd completely glossed over a few key things. "And how exactly will I go about removing a scale from the serpent?"

"That's for you to determine. But I will warn you..." Her eyes darkened. "The serpent is an ancient creature of magic. He has thousands of years of knowledge. If you're unwary, he will trick you, and he would love nothing more than to add your bones to his hoard."

"Will I survive?" I asked bluntly. She knew so much about

me already, there was a good chance she had a better idea of my survival chances than I did.

"Not likely, but there's a small chance you may outsmart him. An exceedingly small chance."

"How lovely." I tapped my fingers on the tabletop. "Why are you bothering to send me if you believe I'll fail?"

"Ah!" Her eyes lit up. "That may be the only intelligent question you've asked. Yes, I do believe you'll fail. No one survives the ice serpent unscathed—if they survive at all. But you're young. You've never faced a real challenge before. I won't know your true potential until you're put to a test. Now." She straightened her dress, then scooted the book toward me. "Place your hand on the page, and I will speak the incantation to send you to the Ice Realm."

I crossed my arms. This all seemed overly hasty and convenient. Plus, the witch admitted to knowing I would come to her. I was beginning to believe she'd sent the wyvern into our village. Maybe she'd enchanted it to attack Father. She knew nothing could cure him but her magic. Maybe it was a giant leap to suspect such a thing, but she did have an unusual interest in my powers and potential. What better way to test me than to attack my father?

"No," I answered. "Not until you tell me why you're so interested in my abilities. Is it because of my skill to heal animals?"

"That has nothing to do with it." She waved at me dismissively. "And don't bother pressing me with more questions because I refuse to answer. Place your hand on the book as I've instructed."

I frowned. I would be going without weapons or provisions. How long would I be there? If I died, how would my family know? This was beginning to look like a horrible plan. Plus, she was wrong about me.

"It's not true that I've never faced any real challenges. If you claim to know so much about me, you would realize it. I watched my own mother die at the hands of the Drau, watched my castle burn in dragon fire. I've lived my life as a thief and a recluse because of what they did to me. Don't pretend to know me when you don't."

Without another word, I stepped to the book and placed my hand on it.

～

THE COLD CAME as a shock to my senses. Freezing wind funneled around me, deafening, though somewhere in the distance, I heard the witch's voice.

"Ash!" her voice echoed. "Ash, you daft beast. Away from the book... Away!"

The wind stopped, and I laid face down in the snow. Bile rose to my throat, and I thought I might be sick. Had I really made it to the Ice Realm? I glanced up, and nothing but a white void spun in my vision. A thousand needles prickled at my skull.

"Ouch," I muttered, resting my head on my arm. The witch could have warned me that going through a portal would make me feel like death.

A wet nose nudged my hand. I looked up to see a pair of cat's eyes peering into mine.

"Ash," I attempted to speak, but the air froze in my lungs. "You... you laid on the book when the witch cast the spell... didn't you?" My head still throbbing, I managed to push to a sitting position, then I took a few deep breaths, and the pain began to fade. "You got sucked into the portal with me, you silly creature." I patted his head, and he mewled. "Or maybe you knew I needed company and decided to come along. Even so, I doubt you'll enjoy our journey. I hope you've got some magic spells ready to go. We'll need them here."

I glanced at the cave's entrance. Inky blackness spanned into the craggy mountainside. Chills prickled my skin as the flow of magic wafted to me. Its power stretched like reaching tendrils, testing my magical senses, and gauging my abilities.

Stars spun in my vision as I got to my feet. My headache turned to a dull throbbing, and I did my best breathe deeply until it relented. Ash trotted beside me as I trudged through powdery snow to the cave's entrance. An icy wind blustered, cutting straight to my bones.

I hugged my arms around myself as best as I could, fearing I would freeze before I even entered the cave. When I finally reached the entrance, my fingers had grown numb, and my ears ached at the icy bite of cold. I rubbed my hands together, taking a moment to observe my surroundings, though there wasn't much to see but a dark tunnel stretching into the mountain.

"No time to waste," I said to Ash, then hiked deeper inside the cave where the world grew silent. Magically glowing ice crystals sprouted along our path, giving us light. The passageway seemed to stretch forever.

"What do you know of this serpent?" I asked Ash to distract me from the silence.

He only trotted alongside me, focused on the path ahead, without paying me any attention.

"I suppose it's a formidable enemy since it's been alive for so long. Do you think I'll have to kill it to get a scale? Or perhaps he'll have shed recently. I can snatch a scale from his discarded skin and be out without ever encountering the beast." I sighed. "But I guess that would be too easy."

I rubbed at a knot in my neck, my thoughts turning back to Father who lay dying on his bed when I'd left him. He'd smiled as I held his hand and told him of my plan. Of course, he always smiled when I told him of my plans. Father was a funny person. He'd grown fat in his old age, and he laughed and joked every chance he got. He loved his family fiercely, although after remarrying Vina, and inheriting three stepsons, I feared he would grow distant from me.

He hadn't. If anything, I think he sensed a possible strain on our relationship, so he'd tried even harder to be close to me whenever he could.

Still, I was nearly twenty-two now. Hardly his little girl anymore. A year ago, I'd moved out of the castle caverns and settled into one of the only remaining towers.

I'd made my home there. Sure, it was lonely at times, but I enjoyed the solitude up in my tower. Plus, Father didn't admit it, but I knew he needed his space with his new bride and stepsons.

I shook my head and focused on the present. The corridor grew narrower, and I found myself crawling on hands and knees through the mud. I envied Ash, who fit through the tiny spaces without a hitch.

As I stood after crawling through a narrow tunnel, I wiped the grime from my hands and knees. The crystals grew taller here, some taller than me. Their glowing bluish lights illuminated the cavernous dome above.

"Well... we made it. Wherever we are. Don't you think it's beautiful, Ash?"

The lights reflected in his luminous eyes, and he only twitched his tail, as if impatient with me.

I continued down the path, the crystals giving me light. Ash stopped in places to sniff rocks or ice crystals, but he always caught up. I half wondered if the witch weren't using him as a spy. It wouldn't be surprising. I'd sensed magic in him. Who knew what sorts of powers he possessed?

Even so, I was glad to have his company.

The sound of running water came from ahead, and I stopped to listen. "That must be the river," I mused to myself. "Come on, Ash, let's find it."

The cat stayed a few paces behind me as I hiked into another chamber. A river of inky black water churned ahead. White caps peeked from the roiling surface.

I picked my way over the rocks as I followed along its shore, slipping a few times on slime-covered stones. In some places, glowing white starfish were stuck to the pebbles, and tiny crystals grew between the cracks. Black sand covered the ground ahead, and I traded the rocks for level ground to avoid falling. My boots made impressions in the soft sand, and Ash left his prints beside mine. My tracker's brain worried at leaving the signs of our passing, but I was surely overreacting. Too much time spent sneaking through the Drau city had left me paranoid.

I was the best thief in the village, which was why the villagers chose me to steal dragon eggs. We needed them to fuel our magic, which left us in a vicious cycle of stealing eggs for survival—and stealing them from the Drau, no less. So far, I'd escaped detection, but how long could my luck last?

I clutched the pendant around my neck. Its magic warmed me and gave me power, but it was a temporary enchantment. Soon, our magic would wane as the egg's power ran dry, and I'd have to return to the city and steal another egg.

But those were worries for another day.

The rush of water grew louder. Spray misted the air and coated my skin as we approached a wooden-planked bridge. It spanned a crevasse so deep I couldn't see the bottom. I kicked a rock and launched it over the edge, then listened for the sound of it hitting bottom.

"...four, five, six, seven..." I counted to myself, until I heard a faraway clatter when I reached eleven.

"Think you'd land on your feet if you jumped down there?" I asked Ash, who only gave me a sullen yawn, revealing a set of impressively sharp teeth. "Right, guess I'd better not test it."

I squared my shoulders and faced the bridge. Boards were missing in places, and others dangled from the worn ropes. A nervous lump tightened in my throat. I'd never been a fan of heights. But maybe I could repair the bridge? If so, how? Magic, of course, but I would have to be smart about it and do it without using up my own powers before encountering the serpent.

I glanced at the cat sitting by me, who was daintily licking his paw, so I bent and picked him up, then cradled him to my chest. "Good kitty," I said, scratching behind his ears. "I need you to use your magic to repair the bridge."

He hung limply in my arms.

"Try it," I nudged, holding him toward the abyss.

He let out a long *meow* and leapt out of my arms. I placed my hands on my hips as he sat and scratched his ear. "Why did you bother to come if you refuse to help me? You could at least be useful and fix the bridge, or magically transport us across the gap... or... or something!"

He yawned.

"Okay. I get." I was tempted to steal some of his magic. Just a little. But what if the witch found out? And what if his powers turned out to be so volatile, I destroyed the cavern? No. Stealing his power wasn't an option either.

I turned and faced the bridge. Maybe I'd imagined he had magic. Maybe he was an ordinary housecat after all. If that were the case, then I'd have to do this the old-fashioned way.

"I'm doing this for Father," I reminded myself, then I took the first step onto the bridge.

It wobbled dangerously, and I held tightly to the ropes on either side of me, my feet planted on the first board.

"This is ridiculous," I mumbled as I took another step, then another. Ash stayed seated on solid ground behind me.

Near the middle of the bridge, several of the planks were missing, leaving a gap wider than I could jump.

My only option was to hold to the ropes and shimmy across hand over hand. It was stupid dangerous. But I didn't see any alternatives at this point.

"Fine," I sighed in resignation, tightening my hands on the ropes. "Here goes nothing." I grasped the ropes and shuffled across hand over hand. Rough fibers burned my palms. Sweat slicked my fingers. My muscles screamed as I moved an inch, then another. When I neared the next plank, I attempted to swing my legs onto it, but the motion made me lose my grip.

I screamed as I held to the rope with one hand. The nearly bottomless abyss spun in my vision. Across the way, Ash sat primly on the ledge as I clawed my way to the plank. Gasping for breath, I managed to snag my boot's toe on the board. I hung precariously, one hand on the rope, a toe on the plank, and tried not to panic.

"I can do this," I breathed. With another kick, I planted my foot on the board, then climbed onto the bridge, holding to the ropes for dear life. Sweat covered my skin in a clammy sheen. My heart thundered, and blood raced through my veins.

I crawled until I reached the other side. When I touched solid ground, I collapsed, staring at the ceiling overhead. My muscles burned and my head throbbed, but I'd made it across.

A blur of gray caught my attention, and I sat up in time to see Ash bounding from plank to plank. When he reached the missing section, he didn't hesitate to leap gracefully across, land on the opposite side, and continue until he reached me.

"Show off," I said between breaths as I climbed to a sitting position, then rubbed the stinging blisters on my palms. Everything ached, and I almost reconsidered my decision to come here. But how could I think such a thing?

Father needed me. The healers had tried their best to cure him, but at this point, all they were doing was making him comfortable until he died. It wouldn't happen. I would get the serpent's scale or die trying—which was a likely outcome at this point.

"I won't give up this easily," I said as I stood.

Ash trailed me as I took the path leading through the stone formations. Stalactites hung like chandeliers from the ceiling, and stalagmites grew pillar-like from the ground. A few glowing crystals dotted our path. The river ran through a deep gorge below us, and I continued following it through the cavern. The distant sound of running water chased me.

I walked until my feet ached and my stomach rumbled with hunger pains. We must've been trekking through the tunnel for hours when I came upon a giant doorway blocking my path.

Runes etched the stone barrier, although I couldn't read the language.

"What's this?" I mused.

Ash sniffed the door, then sat and flicked his tail.

Squaring my shoulders, I faced the door. "What are the chances I can just push it open?"

I placed my hand on the surface and pushed. It didn't budge. I shoved harder, but knew it was useless.

Sighing in frustration, I stepped away from the door. "The witch didn't mention anything about a sealed door, did she?"

I rubbed the sore muscles in my neck. There had to be a way through, and my bet was the runes had something to do with it. I'd studied a little of the ancient languages, and some of the characters looked familiar.

One character, a line that branched into three separate lines at the top, represented magic.

Most likely the door needed my magic to function, but I hesitated to use my powers. What if the door's enchantment stole what little magic I had before I even confronted the serpent? But unless I got through this door, I'd never get the chance to confront it, let alone take one of its scales.

"Here goes," I breathed, then closed my eyes and released the pendant's magic. Its power flowed into me, then extended into my arms and brushed my fingertips.

When I was ready, I opened my eyes. My hands glowed with a soft bluish hue. Breathing deeply, I pressed my hands to the door. Magic flowed from my fingertips and into the stone. It pulled at me, sucking my power from me ever so gently.

Dizziness clouded my head. My vision faded and knees buckled.

I must've fallen to the ground, because the last thing I remember seeing was Ash standing over me, looking at me with his wide yellow eyes.

"Meow..." came a sound from far away. "Meoowww..." the sound came louder and more demanding.

I groaned as I opened my eyes. Every muscle in my body protested. If I'd been hit by a bolt of lightning, this was what it would feel like. Moving hurt. Breathing hurt. Everything hurt. What had happened?

A hint of a blue glow gave me just enough light to see the rock formations overhead. Cool cavern air washed over me. I tilted my head. The giant stone doorway stood open, revealing a passageway lined in shimmering ice crystals.

My heart leapt in my chest. I'd done it! I'd opened the door.

But at what cost? I took several deep breaths through the pain, then I sat up. I opened and closed my hands, and my joints ached. A faint glow of magic warmed my chest, so small I could barely discern it. I clutched my pendant, and it no longer illuminated my hand. Ash brushed against me, purring, and I patted his head.

"That was a mistake," I whispered to him. "The doorway stole almost every ounce of my magic. I'm lucky to be alive." I bit my bottom lip as I mulled over what might have caused the door to react in such a way. Perhaps it was enchanted to take a person's magic, ensuring that whoever tried to enter would be rendered useless.

Hmm. So, it was a safety precaution. And without my powers, my only defense against a snow serpent was a flimsy knife tucked in my boot.

Here's to hoping he was friendly.

When I stood up, I had to steady myself to keep my balance. It felt as if the rocks beneath my feet had turned to shifting sand. The world tilted from side to side, and I placed my hand on the cavern's wall to keep from falling.

Ash rubbed against my legs and looked up at me, as if encouraging me to keep going. I took a step forward, then entered the ice cavern.

Chill air blasted me and came as a shock. I rubbed my hands over my arms to generate some warmth, but it didn't stop the chill bumps from raising on my skin. The cold turned my breath to puffs of white steam.

Ahead, I spotted a raised platform. A giant gray snake lay coiled atop it.

My heart leapt into my throat.

Was I ready to confront the creature?

Yes, I told myself. *You've come too far. You can't fail Father now.*

I neared the serpent, and the creature remained motionless. A chandelier of ice glowed overhead, shining on the serpent's sloughing scales. As I approached, musical tinkling resounded from the chandelier, and its light refracted around the cavern, painting prisms on the stone walls.

Ash padded on quiet feet beside me, his tail twitching, while I circled the snake. Coils lay statue-like on the platform.

Its scales tempted me. I clutched my hands, imagining removing one of the scales and escaping this place. After curing Father, my world would be as it should. I would have a life with Father in it.

Tears pricked my eyes as a wave of sadness washed over me. I'd been so focused on saving him, I hadn't pondered the alternative. If he died, what then?

Losing him meant I never got to sit next to him while we ate our dinner of fresh bread and wild mushroom stew, a fire glowing in the hearth, illuminating the wrinkles on his careworn face. It meant I never got to hear his deep belly laughter again. It meant he would never again tell his stories of the wars. I'd been so terrified of the dragon that had nearly killed him, taking his leg and an eye in the process. Father had survived so much. It seemed unreal to lose him now.

The head of the serpent came into view. Dull scales peeled from the serpent's face, and opened wounds wept pus from gashes in its flesh. Glassy white eyes seemed to peer straight through me, as if the creature couldn't see me.

I stopped short, a shiver going down my spine at the intensity I felt in its presence.

Magic emanated from the animal. The energy surrounded me, deep and oppressive, making it hard for me to draw in a breath. This was an old, pure form of magic.

But a sense of excruciating pain tugged at me. I reached out and touched the snake's face. Cold pierced straight to my heart. Overwhelming sadness engulfed me, as if the creature were crying out for help. Torment racked its body, and I knew its death was imminent. Within days. Hours, perhaps. Not even the strength of its own magic could keep it alive much longer.

I ripped my hand from its face.

Tears pricked my eyes, and I hastily wiped them away. It was as if the universe were pleading with to me to save the beast. But how could I?

No matter how much regret I might have felt later, I couldn't let this creature's death distract me from my purpose. In truth, this was the luckiest scenario possible. I could take a scale and the monster wouldn't have the power to stop me. Father would be saved.

If I chose to heal the snake, then what? The witch assured me it would kill me. Healing it meant my death and Father's as well. I would be a fool to let the creature live.

I slipped my fingers into the top of my boot and grasped the hilt of my knife. Standing tall, blade in hand, I faced the serpent. The icy chandelier shone overhead, my blade reflecting its light.

I knew that as soon as my knife slid into its flesh, the pain would be too much, and the beast would die. But this was for the best. Perhaps the animal wished to give its life so Father could live. Yes, maybe that was it.

A scale on the serpent's neck was raised and weeping pus. Prying it free should have been easy enough. I reached for it, intent on removing it and escaping before I could second guess my decision.

Something bumped into my leg, and I hesitated.

Ash peered up at me, his eyes filled with scorn.

"Stay back, Ash," I whispered, my voice echoing through

the domed room. I reached for the snake again when Ash mewled.

"Stop that," I told him. "I have to do this. Father will die unless I take a scale."

With a deep exhale, I placed my knife's tip at the base of the protruding scale.

Ash leapt onto the platform and bumped my hand, moving the knife away from the beast. He twitched his nose, then he nudged my hand. As he touched me, a flash of a memory jolted me.

I stood in the witch's cabin healing Ash's flea bites. It was as if the cat were speaking to me through that memory, like he was reminding me that if I could do something as insignificant as heal the discomfort of a common housecat, then surely, I could restore a creature as noble as the ice serpent.

Indecision warred within me, but only for a moment.

I let my hand fall to my side. My knife dropped to the floor with a resounding clatter.

"You're right, Ash," I said. "I have no choice but to heal the serpent. The world would never be the same without it."

Once more, I reached for the beast, but this time, I held no weapon.

Resting my hand on its forehead, I closed my eyes.

I had no magic left, but this sort of healing had always been with me—a gift I'd had since birth that never depended upon the magic of the dragon's egg. It was a power familiar only to me and no one else.

Taking a deep breath, I summoned the power deep inside me and let the energy flow from me and into the serpent. The magic moved fluidly, a golden ribbon spanning from my fingertips and straight into the heart of the serpent.

The power glowed brighter until the snake's head moved a

fraction of an inch. Smooth, iridescent scales replaced its dull ones. The chandelier's light refracted off its serpentine body, painting rainbows on the walls of ice. The creature's beauty caught me by surprise, and I could do nothing but stare at the majestic being before me. Its face loomed in my vision, mesmerizing. Its eyes were like sparkling diamonds, translucent and glittering.

This was no mere serpent. This was something more, larger than life, one of the Old Ones who came from the beginning.

Its glassy eyes focused. Slit pupils locked on me, and I froze.

"You..." the snake hissed. Its voice resounded deep inside me, as if I heard it with more than my ears, but deep within my soul. It came to me as if it spoke from lifetimes ago, as if it knew me personally. "You healed me?"

I nodded, then moved my hand away. My fingers tingled where I'd touched him.

"Why?" he asked.

"Because..." I tried to answer, but my mind blanked. My voice sounded so small compared to his. I was nothing to him, a speck not worthy to be in his presence. Yet here I was, talking to him and still living. Didn't he deserve an explanation? "Because I couldn't allow you to die."

His face loomed closer. His eyes locked on me. His black slit pupils were superimposed over an ocean of glittering white. I couldn't look away no matter how hard I tried.

"Who are you?" he asked.

Despite the witch's warning about revealing my name, the serpent compelled me to answer. His presence was so powerful, I feared refusing to answer him would end in my death. "My name is Meara Wintersong."

"Me-ara," he repeated slowly. His forked tongue flicked and tasted the air. He shifted his coils, which moved without sound. "Know this. I am the servant of Time, the bringer of

Knowledge, and the wielder of Death. Those who enter my cavern do so at great risk to their own lives."

"I understand," I said.

"No, you do not." His tongue flicked again. "Many souls have perished here. Thousands of souls. In truth, only the witch have I allowed to live. She knew this when she sent you here. She expected your death."

I stood tall. His words shouldn't have surprised me, although knowing he had only allowed *one* person to live among the thousands who had come here was a dauting thought, one that made a spike of fear shoot through my heart. "Are you going to kill me like you did the others?"

"Indeed, I could." His eyes gleamed. "Should I consume you, your magic would become mine. I could live for centuries more with your healing powers flowing through my blood. However." He hesitated. "You healed me of your own accord, and I am compelled to repay the debt. Since you saved my life, I must spare yours. Tell me, why have you sought me out?"

I stood tall, although my heart was beating frantically. Yes. He was powerful, but I wouldn't let him intimidate me. "I've come for one of your scales."

His laughter echoed around the cavern. "Bold words. Most who come here are too afraid to speak the desire of their heart, but you beg for one of my scales without hesitancy. Why?"

"Because of my father. He was attacked by a wyvern. Only a potion made from your scale can heal him."

He tilted his head. "Yes, I sense your fear of losing him. But death is a natural part of life. All die. You must not fear death."

"Yes, you're right. But I need him. He's my father, and he's the king—or he was. I need him, and our people need him. Now more than ever. We'll take our revenge on the Drau and restore our kingdom to its former—"

"No..." the snake stopped me. "The time of the Encantasians has passed. Your demise at the hands of the dragons was prophesied. There is no return for your people."

I swallowed a nervous lump in my throat, and my stomach soured. "Then we're doomed to live as vagrants for the rest of our lives?"

"That is not what I said."

"Maybe not, but what other future do we have?"

"That is for you to discover," he answered, his eyes narrowed.

I crossed my arms, unnerved at the idea of my people never being restored. I was five when the dragons had descended on our city and decimated it, leaving my home in ruins. Those who survived the attack were left to live as nomads in the ruins of our once great castle. Nothing had been the same since then. But I'd come here for another reason. I squared my shoulders and fisted my hands. Maybe saving my people wouldn't happen today, but saving my father was another story.

I would just have to find a way to reason with the serpent.

"Then help me save my father," I said. "I know he's going to die someday, but he's not ready to go yet. You don't understand. He's the only parent I've got. He's a good man, and he was a good king. He's got a good heart and a noble soul."

The snake only stared at me with his strange diamond eyes. "I can see many things. He keeps a great secret from you."

Irritation simmered in my chest, and I crossed my arms, unnerved at his accusation. "Even if that's true, it makes no difference. I can't watch my father die. Don't you understand? I need him!" Tears pricked my eyes, and I blinked to keep them from running down my face. The passion in my voice surprised even me. Yes, I knew I loved my father and wanted him to live. But perhaps I'd never realized how much I loved him until this moment.

Did it matter that he kept secrets from me? Maybe. But

everyone had their secrets, and if Father hid something from me, he must have had his reasons.

"Indeed, I see you care deeply for your father." He spoke softly, as if perhaps he understood my emotions. Did such a creature have any concept of family? If so, then he must have known the pain I was experiencing. "I will allow you to have one scale from my flesh. Your father will be cured. But be warned, not all is as it seems. Much calamity awaits you." A red sheen glossed over the serpent's eyes. The cavern dimmed, and a slight tremor rumbled under my feet. "Taking this scale alters your future. You will gain heavy burdens, some that will seem unbearable. Receiving this scale means you will trade who you believe you need most..." His face loomed so close I could see gold flecks in his eyes... "for who you will hold most dear."

What did he mean by that? Who I held most dear? I held Father most dear. No one in my life meant more than him. But he'd said who I *would* hold most dear.

Queasiness filled my stomach, and I had to swallow a wave of nausea.

What if I did something now that I would regret later?

But could I really let those thoughts worry me? The serpent may have known much, but he didn't know everything. Like the witch, he didn't know me. The future hadn't been written yet.

Leaving this cavern without the scale would be something I would forever regret. I would never forgive myself for allowing Father to die when I could have saved him. When the future came, I would deal with it, and I wouldn't worry about it until then.

The serpent loomed over me.

Sharp diamond eyes peered into mine as he uncoiled. The

serpent hissed, then opened his mouth to reveal fangs dripping with venom.

Was he going to attack me?

I clenched my fists. Instinctively, I reached for my magic, only to find a cold spot where the warmth of my magic once resided. Clutching my pendant, I took a deep breath. If he killed me, there was nothing I could do to stop him. But what reason did he have to kill me? No. This wasn't meant as a show of aggression. I wouldn't fear him.

"You have cured me," the serpent said. "I will give you the desire of your heart. Your wish is granted, Meara Wintersong."

He raised one of his coils, then something silvery fell to the ground with a soft thud.

A scale lay on the ground, shimmering with a pearly irides-cent beauty that made me catch my breath.

I stared in shock at the object, as if it weren't real, but then I picked it up, and its magic called to me.

Warmth enveloped me. My magic returned, filling the empty spaces inside my soul.

"You've been warned," the snake said, coiling once again to sleep on his dais.

Holding the scale, I stood unmoving. Its power enshrouded me in a warm cocoon, and I was sure I'd never felt so at peace.

But I had a mission to accomplish, and I couldn't stand here forever enamored by the scale. I tucked the object in the pouch at my waist, grabbed my knife, and left the cavern and the serpent behind, Ash trailing at my feet.

I KNELT by Father's bedside and raised the flask to his mouth. After escaping the serpent's cavern, I'd returned to the witch's hut. She'd fulfilled her promise and given me the healing potion. All was well, or at least, it should have been.

The serpent's warning nagged me. What secret did Father keep from me?

Liquid trickled into his mouth, and Father swallowed. His eyes remained closed, and his face unnaturally pale, so I grasped his hand in mine. Several healers and my stepmother gathered around us.

Flames flickered in sconces from the roughly hewn walls. Garlands had been strung along the walls in preparation for the festival of the winter solstice. Despite the cheerfulness of the greenery, the castle's dungeons caged me in. Water dripped somewhere in the distance. Being confined in the bowels of the old castle did nothing to help restore Father's health, but no one ventured above ground for fear of dragon attacks. Well, no one but me. I'd decided to make my home atop the highest tower left in the old palace. Perhaps I didn't fear dragons as I should have, or perhaps I feared them and didn't care.

Whatever the case, my place in this moment was here with Father. I had worked so hard to find a cure for him. I wanted nothing more than to see him open his eyes. Seeing him smile would be nice, too. I would do anything just to see his smile again.

"Tell me again how you came upon the potion?" my stepmother asked. Dark circles ringed her eyes. She wore a wimple that covered most of her hair, though a few strands of brunette and gray peeked from the cloth. Splotches spotted her aging face. She wrung her hands, her bones protruding from her thin skin.

"I got a scale from an ice serpent," I answered for the third time since I'd entered the castle tunnels, trying my best to be patient with her. She wasn't daft. In fact, she was an intelligent woman, yet I suspected she was wary of my story. I had to admit, it was a bit unbelievable. "I traded it for the witch's potion."

"But how?" she asked, her voice hitching. "An ice serpent? Do they even exist? And how did you survive the witch? Everyone knows how dangerous she is."

Father coughed, which kept me from having to come up with answers to her list of questions.

"Father," I said gently, then patted his shoulder. "Can you hear me?"

He opened his mouth and breathed deeply. "Meara," he whispered, his voice hoarse. "Is that you?"

"Yes. It's me. I'm here, Father."

He coughed again. "That drink..." he licked his dry, cracked lips. "Terrible. Why would you give your poor father such a nasty draught?"

Ah, Father. Barely conscious and still joking around with me. It warmed my heart to hear his voice. "It woke you up, didn't it?"

Finally, he opened his one good eye. "Yes, I'm awake, though I imagine you could wake the dead with that foul drink."

My stepmother clasped her hands under her chin and knelt on the opposite side of the bed from me. "Herrald, thank the gods. You're alive."

"Aye, Vina. By the gods, I don't know how. But I'm alive."

"It was Meara," she answered, dabbing a tear from her eye. "Your blessed daughter saved you, praise be. Oh, Meara." She reached across the bed and grasped my fingers. "I still don't understand how you managed it, but you've saved him."

Murmurs came from the people surrounding us. Their excited whispers carried through the room, and someone left to carry the news to the rest of the people. "The king lives," I heard someone say.

Father grasped my hand and squeezed my fingers. His blue eye, a match to mine, softened as he looked at me. "I should be dead, Meara. That wyvern venom was enough to finish me off. It's a miracle that I'm talking to you and not on a floating pyre headed out to be greeted by the great Sea Goddess. I hardly expected to make it to the winter solstice festival. How in Encantasia did you manage to save me?"

I swallowed a nervous lump in my throat. Should I tell him the truth? Admit that I'd taken a scale from the serpent and altered the path of my future? And that wasn't even the worst of it. "The witch helped me," I said quietly.

His eyes widened. "You went to her?"

I nodded.

"That was more than just risky. It was foolish. You could have been on that pyre along with me sailing to see the goddess."

"I know, but you don't understand how helpless I felt. I knew while you lived, there was a chance you could be saved. I would do anything to save you. Even pay a visit to the witch. She didn't kill me, and I saved you, so there's no need for alarm, is there?"

He shook his head. "You have no idea the danger you put yourself in." He closed his eye and muttered something unintelligible. "...*Evalon* ...." He whispered the name, and I almost didn't catch it. "*Evalon,*" he whispered again.

A current of magic rippled through the air at the mention of the name. A jolt of electricity shot through me.

The name sounded so eerily familiar, as if I'd heard it once, long ago. But when?

A memory surfaced. A woman wearing a fur-lined hood stood in the forest. She carried a basket on her arm. I'd seen her once, so long ago, and only now did I remember her face. And remember her name...

"Evalon..." Father's voice came as if from ages past.

The witch's words echoed from when I first met her.

Only those acquainted most intimately with me know my name.

Suspicions collided, and my imagination took me to places I'd rather not go.

What was Father keeping from me? Should I dare ask him?

Healers bustled around him, and my stepmother sat looking on him with adoring eyes.

Gently, I moved my hand away from his shoulder and stood.

I dare not ask such personal questions to him now, not with everyone around, not for a secret as big as this.

Maybe he couldn't tell me, but perhaps someone else would be willing to speak the truth.

SNOWFLAKES TUMBLED past in a torrent of sparkling white. I once again took the path through the forest to the witch's cabin, although this time, I came for a different reason. My stomach hadn't stopped roiling all night, and I doubted I'd gotten more than a few hours of sleep. Too many questions nagged at me. The truth of my birth, of my family, and my heritage. Who was I really?

Only one person could give me answers. She hadn't killed me before, and I doubted she'd do it now, especially now that I suspected I knew why she'd spared me to begin with.

It must have been hard to kill your own offspring.

The cabin's door stood ajar, and Ash stood on the threshold. He tilted his head as I approached.

"Hey, Ash." I bent and rubbed his back.

"You're early again." The voice echoed from behind the cabin. "I didn't expect you for another week at least." I followed the sound, which led me on a path that wound behind the cabin to a small garden. Cardinals fluttered around holly bushes dusted in powdery snow. Poinsettias grew along trellises, and the witch stood holding a basket and a pair of shears as she pruned the plants.

The familiar, floral scent caught me off guard, and a vague memory surfaced from my childhood. I remembered standing in this very spot, clutching Father's hand, and feeling slightly anxious. She'd worn a green dress then, with a fur-lined hood.

The witch snipped a flower's stem, then placed it in her basket.

"You're my mother, aren't you?" I blurted, not caring to mince words, and desperate for the truth, no matter how painful it may have been.

Her mouth curved into a slight smile. "Why would you ever accuse me of such a thing?"

"How did you trick my mother to think I was her own?"

The witch stared at me with a penetrating gaze. The breeze picked up, catching strands of her golden red hair and brushing them over her cheeks. "A witch never reveals her secrets." She spoke with a soft, sad tone. "That's lesson two."

"So, you are my mother."

She didn't answer, which spoke volumes. I didn't pretend to know much about sorcery. Magic, yes. But spells and incantations were another beast altogether. Perhaps she'd used a memory charm to make Mother think I was hers. Whatever the case, I suspected the witch would never outright confirm the truth. And neither would Father.

"Father knew your name. You said only those who were intimately acquainted with you knew it. And the serpent said

Father was keeping a secret from me. You and Father must have sworn to one another never to reveal the truth."

Ash rubbed against my legs as the witch only stared at me, her expression wistful and sad.

"If I'd had a daughter of my own," she finally said. "I would want to teach her all I know of magic. Would you be willing to learn, Meara?"

Yes, I wanted to answer without hesitation. If I could become as powerful as the witch, I would be able to avenge our kingdom and bring justice to our people once and for all. But who would I become if I answered yes? Would I become someone like her? Someone who had no respect for human life?

With so much power, it must have been easy to think of others as mere animals not worth a second thought.

No. I couldn't allow her to train me. At least, not until I knew what I would be getting into, when I'd grown more mature, when it would be easier for me to not confuse wisdom and power.

"Perhaps someday," I answered. "When I'm ready."

She pinched her lips and gave a curt nod, as if not surprised with my answer, but still disappointed. "I understand." She lowered her eyebrows. Her expression turned cold and unfeeling, as if she no longer had use for me. "You should go, young one. Don't return until you have reason."

She turned her back on me. As she faced the trellis, disappointment tugged at me. I'd had the chance to get to know my mother, and I'd refused it, though I knew I'd made the right choice.

I turned to leave.

"Ash," she called over her shoulder, and I stopped. "Go with her. She needs you more than me."

Ash mewled and twitched his tail.

"Go!" she demanded. "I have no more use for you here."

"You're giving me the cat?" I asked.

"Consider it a parting gift, and..." She glanced at me over her shoulder. "It's my way of making sure you're safe." She closed her eyes and heaved a long sigh, as if releasing the weight of the world. Perhaps she finally felt freed from carrying such a great secret for so long. While she hadn't outright confirmed my suspicion, she knew that I knew the truth, which I speculated was enough. "Goodbye, Meara."

Ash purred and rubbed my legs, and I picked him up. The witch wouldn't be training me yet, but she'd be watching me.

"Goodbye," I echoed her, Ash in my arms, as I left the cottage and the witch—my mother—behind.

CHAPTER 3
GIFTS OF THE MAGIC
BY ROBERT A. BROWN AND JOHN WOOLEY

(NOTE: In these letters, the protagonist occasionally refers to his previous adventures as a field writer for the Work Projects Administration, which dispatched him to a remote part of Arkansas to collect tales of folklore. This stretch of Robert's life is chronicled in the Cleansing trilogy: *Seventh Sense, Satan's Swine,* and *Sinister Serpent.*)

December 1, 1939
Friday evening

Dear John,
     As I left Mrs. Dean's boarding house for my job at the cold gray Department of War building this morning, I thought about how you were overdue for a missive from me. I made up my mind to write you today, knowing I'd have to be careful not to blather on again about how hard it is to get to know people here in our nation's capital, especially

when they seem to be nervous all the time, rushing helter-skelter like ants through the city, looking over their shoulders, too busy and maybe too rattled to care about anyone but themselves and what they're doing, deeply suspicious of anyone they don't know. I'm sure that's why it's been so tough to warm up to my fellow boarders – although that might also have to do with the fact that Mrs. Dean's cooking is pretty much for the birds, and she seldom has more than one or two of the four of us at the dining-room table. Hard to get to know people who aren't around you much.

Still, I guess I like it better than the apartment I went to when I first hit town. It's cheaper, and it's quieter, and at least some of us eat together. In the apartment building, we were like strange bees, all going out and then buzzing back every day to our little cells, sealing ourselves up from those on the other sides of our walls.

I guess I really can't blame people around here for being unfriendly and suspicious, though. The whole notion of another world war hangs over everything like black crepe, and it's not doing anybody any good (except for maybe giving guys like me all the work we can handle for 150 frog skins a month).

And here it is December. Christmas is coming, chum, and I just can't _feel_ it like I used to. Peace on earth? Who can buy _that_ nowadays?

So, like I say, I was all prepared to beef to you about how I still don't really have any friends here after pretty near three months in Washington and how the holiday decorations are already up in a lot of the stores, reminding me of our great kid Christmases in Minnesota, and so on and so on and ain't it sad about poor old Robert, an innocent alone and forlorn on the big city streets, pressing his nose against the bright department store windows as he gazes wistfully at the toy trains and the happy little animated figures.

That's probably something like what I was *going* to write. But that changed today.

I don't think I've told you about the dogs in this town. I guess most of 'em are pets, but there are some that just hang around the buildings and look pitiful. You remember me writing you about the experiment that Mr. Destruidora and his daughter put me through back in Arkansas, showing me how to see through the eyes of a coyote? They told me I could do that any time with dogs and coyotes and even wolves if I practiced enough. Well, I kind of halfheartedly tried it a couple of days ago with a friendly, sad-faced mutt that lives in the alley behind the boarding house. I didn't really see anything through his eyes, but I did feel a kind of, I don't know, *kinship* with him that went deeper than just the usual connection between dogs and the people they like and trust. Now, when I get close enough to a dog – which has only happened a couple of times so far – I try to send out a mental link. When I do, I generally get one back. I'll continue to let you know about what happens with this.

I guess I've been doing a lot of mulling on the seventh sense and all that happened to me back in Arkansas. Of course, I've had a lot of time to reflect, since I don't have any pals here yet. (Oops. I told you I wouldn't sound like a wet sock. Sorry.) Last night, I took a break from reading the new *Spider* magazine – "The Spider and the Pain Master," a damn good yarn – to set out my clothes for the next day, and I ran onto that little three-cent piece on a string that the old boy gave me back at Jolley's Mercantile up in the Ozarks. Remember me telling you about it – the "witch-charm" that vibrated whenever evil or the occult was around? I held it in my hand for a little bit, thinking back to my fight with the evilest son-of-a-bitch in that Arkansas town, Old Man Black, and then, hell, I just slipped it over my head and let it dangle from my neck. Somehow, it brought me immediate comfort. I felt then that between my seventh sense and that talisman, I could forestall any threat that might come my way.

Next day at the Department of War, I turned to (as the gobs say), skipping lunch and finishing a stack of orders for the Army. Because I'd gotten my work done so fast, Mr. Fletcher came by my desk at 4:30 and told me I could leave if I wanted to. He's got orang-utan breath and a haircut that makes him look like Moe in the Three Stooges, but I guess he isn't that bad after all. I took the extra half-hour and headed to a nearby department store, where I found and bought a nice Fada radio with a pair of earphones thrown in for cheap. Mrs. Dean has a list of rules a yard long, and No. 3 is no radio after 8 p.m. Of course, no radio means no radio she can _hear_.

Although the street car line runs right by my boarding house, I've been getting off several blocks beforehand and poking around the adjacent neighborhoods on my way home. Today, it was a pretty nice coldish afternoon, not unlike fall in Minnesota, and I felt like walking. There were a few folks out on their porches, but not many, and now that we were out of the city proper the traffic wasn't bad.

By the time I got to the side street that leads to Mrs. Dean's place, there wasn't anyone else out and about. It was tree-lined, dark, and chilly with the approaching evening. Up in front of me about a half-block, shuffling his way along the sidewalk with a box of groceries, I spotted the "boy" at the boarding house, an old gee named Mr. Saki. I'd seen him around and we'd said hello to one another a few times, but that was about it.

At just that time, I felt something funny brushing against my chest, like the legs of skittering insects. It took me a moment to realize it was the witch-charm.

Suddenly alert, I watched as four guys materialized in front of the old man – high school age, from the looks of 'em, big and gangly. I felt my seventh sense rise up, triggered by the fluttering of the talisman, but neither was necessary. I could see immediately that those lads were trouble.

Sure, I didn't really know the old guy from Adam's off ox, but I wasn't going to stand there and watch him get drubbed by four ruffians a third of his age. So I stashed my sack with the radio and phones under a hedge that ran along part of the sidewalk and ran to his aid.

The four had immediately encircled him, jeering and calling him names. He stood straight, not cowering at all, but it was clear he was about to be on the receiving end of a first-class beating. One of them had gotten behind him and I knew that's where I'd better start – especially when that young crumb raised his hand and I saw the unmistakable glint of brass dusters in the fading sunlight. So, just as he swung the knucks downward toward the back of the old man's head, I jumped in and chopped a swift hard jab to his throat. Gagging, he clutched at his neck and slid to the sidewalk. I kicked him one for good measure and when he started throwing up onto the grass I knew he was out of commission. I was aware of shouts and movement behind me, so I whipped around, ready to take on the other three – only to find them laid out like a trio of stiffs in a triple funeral.

You can imagine my surprise. I was wheezing like a radiator from the exertion, but the old Jap wasn't even breathing hard. I know his countrymen have lots of secret hand-to-hand combat styles; I could only figure he'd learned a few.

I looked around. We two vertical combatants and our four horizontal opponents were the only signs of life on the block. I had a feeling – although I don't think it was the seventh sense – that there were people looking out of the windows of the houses around us, unwilling to get involved in this dust-up but maybe more than willing to sic the coppers on us. It was a cold town, I thought, in more ways than one.

"Thank you, young man," he said, bowing. "Robert, isn't it?"

"Right, Mr. Saki," I returned, bending over to pick up the brass knuckles that had slipped off the still-retching assailant's hand. "He was about to crown you with these."

I handed them to him, and he bowed again, slipping them into his pants pocket. "Had you not arrived when you did, it would have been very bad for me."

"I can't argue with that. But maybe we'd better make tracks before someone calls the constabulary." I nodded toward the three unmoving forms in front of him. "I don't know how you did it, but I'm impressed," I told him. "They aren't dead, are they?"

He shook his head and then spit out an epithet that sounded like "banjos."

"Well, that's okay, I guess," I said. "Get going, and I'll catch up with you."

He nodded, bent over to put a few spilled groceries back in his box, and started out at his old-man pace, while I retrieved my sack from under the hedge and trotted up to him.

Suddenly, I thought of that old saw about whether or not a tree that falls in the forest makes a sound if there's no one to hear it. Maybe you could ask the same question about four jackasses who got dropped.

"You are smiling," Mr. Saki said, as we neared the boarding house.

"You bet. I'm happy we didn't have to stick around and answer any questions."

He nodded. After a few more paces, he said, "May I ask why you intervened? I am not used to being helped by one of your race."

"Well, I guess it's like the automobiles at the Indianapolis 500," I said. "They're different colors, but they're all in the same race."

A grin played across his face then, and he stuck out his hand. "I trust you, Robert. You are my friend."

"And you're mine," I said.

He nodded, leaving me at the front door as he made his shuffling way back to his garage apartment, cradling his grocery box.

So now I can finally say I have a friend in Washington, D.C., John.

But I also have to say this: I wonder why I could still feel the three-cent piece fluttering like a sparrow against my chest, stopping only when Mr. Saki was out of my sight?

Your pal and faithful comrade,

Robert

December 4, 1939
Monday evening

DEAR JOHN,

Looks like this friendship with Mr. Saki is already paying off – in spades. Or at least, I hope it is.

I'll explain. Today was another cold and damp day in the Capital of America, and I concentrated on beating my own record on getting orders typed up. I did, and while I didn't say anything to Fletcher about trying to top myself, he was so pleased with my output that he patted me on the shoulder, told me I was a "fine American worker," and told me I could leave a half-hour early again.

I'd been able to get more done by not leaving my desk for lunch; a Coke from the machine on our floor had gotten me through. But I was plenty famished by the time I hit the bricks, so I ankled into a diner up the street and grabbed a hamburger and some thick-cut French fries – a filling meal for 30 cents. Then I hopped onto the trolley, riding it all the way to the boarding house this time. As I headed up the stairs, I waved at Mr. Saki, who was working over the lower floor with a carpet sweeper. He motioned for me to stop.

Walking to the foot of the stairs with that old-man gait of his, he said, "Robert, may I talk with you when I am finished? I have a proposition to discuss."

"Sure," I said.

Satisfied, he returned to his work, and I headed upstairs to my room to get out of my jacket and tie – fully aware that the witch-charm I wore had quivered a bit upon our encounter. When I returned to the bottom floor, I found him mopping the linoleum in the kitchen.

"Let me help," I said. "Make it go quicker."

He looked like he was going to protest, but when I reached for the mop handle, he relented, and while I finished that job he went into the dining room, wiped down the big table, and started setting out plates and silverware. We finished at about the same time, and after he stowed the mop and bucket in a closet, he led me out a side door.

"Thank you, Robert," he said when we were outside, "but, if I may say this, please don't do that again. I think it would make Mrs. Dean very angry if she saw a boarder doing some of my work."

I tried to envision a mad Mrs. Dean, and the mental picture it gave me was the Wicked Witch from *The Wizard of Oz*, sending her monkeys out to snatch up Dorothy and Toto.

"I got you," I said, trying not to give undue notice to the light fluttering of the talisman under my shirt. "Now what about this proposition?"

"Cigarette?" he asked. He produced a pack with Japanese writing on it, shook one out for me, and lit mine and then his. One drag was all it took. It was like inhaling burning socks. So I knocked the fire off and handed it back, making a face and telling him, "A little strong for my taste."

He laughed as he took it and pushed it back in the pack. "All right," he said. "May I tell you now about an American friend of mine who has a niece visiting him for the holidays – a quite attractive young woman?"

"I'm all ears, Mr. Saki."

"He needs some dependable person to entertain her for a few evenings. A dependable person like you, Robert."

Before I could say anything, he went on.

"He will, of course, provide you with ample funds for your meals and entertainment. He's authorized me to give you this as an advance."

With this, he dug into the pocket of his khakis and came up with a wad of bills.

I thought about whistling a few bars of "Just A Gigolo," but I didn't figure he'd get it, so I said, "I'm a full-time employee of the United States Government, Mr. Saki, and I can afford to take a gal on a date. But if it'd make you and your pal happy, sure, I'll spread some of his dough around town."

He actually laughed as I took the money from his hand, stuffing it into my own pocket.

"I don't have an automobile, though," I continued. "Is that a problem?"

"None whatsoever. She has one."

"All right. I'm at your service."

"Shall we say four-thirty Saturday? She can meet you right outside."

"Sure," I told him. "If she's as pretty as you say she is,

maybe it'll make the other boarders jealous. And I guess I should know her name, huh?"

He grinned. "Dianna – with two n's – Jones. I think you will enjoy her company."

With that, he turned and headed toward his garage apartment, still smiling.

Mr. Saki is a man of few words. But he sure sets off my witch-charm. It kept up its gentle thrumming until he was completely out of my sight.

Your pal and faithful comrade,

Robert

December 5, 1939
Tuesday

DEAR JOHN,

Some sort of front has blown through town and it's colder than Little Nell. I know because I've just got out of it and back into my warm-as-toast room.

Old Fletch the Wretch let me go at 4:30 again today. I guess my work habits have kind of made me his pet. So I headed off through this frigid, cloudy Tuesday to Hy's Clothes for Men, the store I've written you about. I needed some new duds for my upcoming date, so I visited Mr. Hiram Gold once again and, about a half-hour later, left 67 dollars lighter but with a real nice suit and some dress shirts – all of it at the "special customer discount" of ten percent that he always extends to me. I needed new shoes to go with the suit, and he suggested Florsheim Shoes, which happened to be next door. He probably gets a little rake-off from sending customers there, but that's all right. I got a good-looking pair of kicks along with new socks for six bucks fifty and tax.

Now, I'm all set for Saturday night, and what I hope will be a lovely girl and a lovely time – all thanks to our "boy" Mr. Saki.

I've been thinking some about him, and why my witch-charm triggers whenever he's around – even though my seventh sense doesn't. What I've come to suspect is that while the old guy may do some fooling around with magic and the occult – something that would set the charm off – I don't get the sense that any particular threat to me personally. So the talisman tells me he's a magic man, and my seventh sense – or lack of it – around him tells me I'm not in any danger from him.

That's the way I've got it figured, anyway. I'm still going to keep a wary eye out– even though the last thing this city needs is someone else viewing others with suspicion.

Your pal and faithful comrade,

Robert

December 9, 1939
Late Saturday night (technically, Sunday morning)

DEAR JOHN,

Well, it is after midnight in our nation's capital, so this will be short. But I feel real good as well as a little bit mixed up, like I was back in high school or something and fell for a new and mysterious girl. (And never mind that we didn't get many of those at Hallock High while we were there.)

As you might have guessed, I had a grand time on the date. Dianna is a swell girl – _unusual_, but swell. And she _is_ a looker, with silky brownish-red hair, big brown eyes, and a solid chassis. She rolled up in front of my place right on time, in a new Nash Ambassador four-door sedan, stepped out to meet me in a plum-colored night-on-the-town dress, offered me her hand as she introduced herself, and asked if I would mind driving. All of that was jake with me, of course.

Mr. Saki had made dinner reservations for us at a hoity-toity restaurant called the Golden Eagle, but they were for seven p.m., so we had a couple of hours to look around the town. That was also Mr. Saki's idea; he told me she hadn't been in Washington before and was curious about the landmarks. So I drove us to the Washington Monument, and we climbed the stairs. Feminine as she was, Dianna had plenty of grit; she went right up that 500-foot staircase in her high-heeled shoes without even getting winded. In fact, she led _me_ most of the way. I was impressed.

After that, we went to the Lincoln Memorial, which didn't seem to make much of an impact on her. I said something to her about how great Lincoln was and didn't she agree? She just sort of nodded. At first, I thought she might be a stars-and-bars Southerner – even though she doesn't have any kind of accent to suggest that – but then I got an odd feeling that maybe she didn't exactly know who Lincoln _was._ That's strange, I know, but that's the impression I got. Instead of being from the South, maybe she's from another country or something. But the few times I tried to ask her about her background she played it real close to the vest, not really telling me anything that would help.

At dinner, I came right out and asked where she was from. But she just met my eyes with those big brown glims of hers, smiled like a heroine in a movie, and said, "It's a little complicated, Robert. I'd rather find out about _you._" So I told her about Minnesota and a little about my CCC days (nothing, of course, about the seventh sense or the darker parts of my Arkansas experiences), hoping that my being forthcoming might help her open up a little. But I ended up doing most of the talking.

About all I could get out of her was that she had been "tutored" and not attended any kind of public school.

The Golden Eagle was decorated with strings of lights crisscrossing the ceiling and wrapped around the railings, twinkling everywhere. At the end of the long bar was a little classy looking fir tree, maybe three feet tall, adorned with more lights and lots of ornaments. It. seemed to really catch her attention. She walked to the tree, squeezed the needles between her thumb and forefinger, and sniffed at the pine scent, like she was inhaling perfume – eyes closed, a smile on her face.

"Looks to me like you're a big fan of Christmas," I said.

She opened her eyes, still smiling, and looked me squarely in the face.

"What I know of it," she said. "I'd like to know more."

Yes, that was another odd thing for her to say, but I chalked it up to her "tutored" education and secretly felt thankful that her comment gave us something else to talk about.

John, your ears were probably burning a few hours ago, as I told her about some of the Christmases we'd had as kids, going out to our little church on Christmas Eve, walking down the street together as snow fell around us, looking at all the lights people had put up across town, feeling full of joy and peace and happiness.

She seemed awfully interested, like she was hanging on every word. Or maybe she was just being polite. But I don't think so. She came up with a lot of questions.

Somewhere in there, we got our menus and she asked me to order a steak for her. There was a porterhouse on the menu, and I had the geetus for it, thanks to Mr. Saki and my anonymous benefactor, so that's what she got. As for me – once I saw frog legs listed I didn't need to see anything else. You know I love 'em, but I've found that they disgust some women, so I felt like I ought to ask her if it would be all right for me to order up a plateful.

"Oh, of course," she said. "I fancy them myself – but they're so hard to catch."

I wasn't sure what to make of that. Maybe a clue that she grew up out in the country somewhere? I do know that she wanted me to make sure her porterhouse was "very rare," and it was. I fact, it was bloody. I was ready to send it back for a little more heat, but she said no and proceeded to eat it with a gusto that surprised me.

But then, Dianna Jones is a surprising young filly. After dinner, I took her to the Empire Theatre to see _Mr. Smith Goes to Washington_, which of course has been making a lot of noise here in the capital since the Press Club premiered it back in October. Knowing she was new to Washington, I thought the movie might help her understand how things work here, and while she was attentive enough throughout the feature – and the cartoon, and the newsreel, and the coming attractions, and a two-reeler called "Glove Slingers" with a couple of good character actors, Noah Beery Jr. and Shemp Howard, the goofy guy from the Joe Palooka shorts – she seemed . . ._confused_ afterward. In fact, as we talked, I got the feeling she not only didn't know any of the basics about the workings of our government, but also about boxing, which was the basis of "Glove Slingers." In her own languid way, she hit me with question after question. What was Mr. Smith doing, talking so long to the other lawmakers? Why didn't the radio and newspapers let people know what he was doing? And was it true that people went to places where they watched men hit each other with those big gloves? She asked questions all the way back to my boarding house, and when we got there she asked a few more.

It was clear that her "tutors," whoever they were, had left some holes in her education.

"I like going to the movies with you," she said. "Will you take me again next Saturday?"

I looked at her there in the half-light, reclining against the Nash's seat. A sharp icy wind swept around the car, but even with the motor off, we were plenty warm.

"You bet," I said.

"Same time?"

"Sure." I checked my strap watch, saw that it was after midnight. "I'd better go before Mrs. Dean comes out to break us up. She's got eyes like a hawk and ears like a burro, and she doesn't like anything untoward going on around her place at this time of night."

She smiled. "I understand."

John, as intoxicating as this woman was, I hadn't made a pass at her the whole time we were together. In fact, I'd been a perfect gentleman. But as I clicked open the driver's-side door, she suddenly grabbed my head with both of her hands and fed me a kiss that packed a real wallop. It was unreal, but nice; I was still feeling it when she pulled away in the sedan.

Then, the two-cent piece, quiet all night, began thrumming under my shirt.

"Was she as you expected, Robert?"

The voice came out of the darkness, and I turned to see Mr. Saki, one of those vile Jap cigarettes stuck in the corner of his mouth. *What a strange way to put it*, I thought.

"She was delightful, Mr. Saki. We got in some sight-seeing, had a nice dinner, and took in *Mr. Smith Goes to Washington* at the Empire. I think she had a good time. In fact, we have a date for next Saturday night."

"A date?" he said, frowning. "Oh, yes, yes. Dates." He brightened then, as though he'd just remembered what the word meant. "Forgive me for asking, but is your money holding up adequately? I have more for you when you need it."

"I'm fine, Mr. Saki. Thanks."

Bowing slightly, he turned toward his garage apartment. After a couple of steps, he stopped and faced me again. "I hope you found her ... well, as you've found other women."

Even in the darkness, I guess he could see the quizzical look on my face, because he quickly added, "My apologies. I am not expressing myself correctly. My friend and I, we are afraid that she may not be like other women. She has lived a very sheltered life. We just want assurance that she is ... *normal*."

"I wouldn't worry about that, Mr. Saki," I told him. "She may be a little more unusual than the run-of-the-mill, but as far as I'm concerned, that just makes her more interesting."

He half-bowed again and walked away. The two-cent piece stopped fluttering against my chest. I went upstairs to my room and started writing this letter, and now you're caught up.

Your pal and faithful comrade,

Robert

December 16, 1939
Early Sunday morning

DEAR JOHN,

I have tried to sleep but I'm not having much luck, so I'm up now, shades drawn, at the typer, in the hope that writing you about what I experienced just a few hours earlier will be cathartic for me. I just hope the clacking of the keys doesn't wake anyone up.

I'd been looking forward to my second date with Dianna since – well, since the first one was over about a week ago. During the last few days, I found myself thinking about her a lot. Sure, I hardly know her, but she's starting to edge herself into my dreams and plans, whether she knows it or not.

I've even thought about calling her, just to talk. I don't know her number, but I'm sure Mr. Saki would give it to me. Then again, we've only had one date, and I don't want her, or Mr. Saki, or his friend, to think I'm a wolf. Plus, the only Ameche I've got access to is the one on the wall downstairs, and I don't think I'd want everyone in the boarding house to hear what I had to say to her.

I've told you that Dianna didn't seem to know some of the basic things about life in America, how our politics work, what Christmas means to us – even what our entertainment is like. She told me, when we went out this time, that she hadn't seen many movies at all.

Maybe that helps explain what happened. Those of us who are used to the flying tintypes don't understand the effect they can have on someone who hasn't been around 'em much.

Here's how it went: She showed up right on time and even surprised me with a quick kiss hello before I got behind the wheel and we took off, ready to dispense with the rest of the lettuce Mr. Saki gave me last week. We ate at the Golden Eagle again, each with the same entree – a blood-rare porterhouse for her, frog legs for me. She even sampled one of my frog legs this time but made a face and pronounced it "too salty." She also had to go back and visit the little Christmas tree at the end of the bar, watching it as the little lights flicked on and off. It seemed to delight her once again. I think she even whispered something to it.

Then, it was off to the movies. This time, we hit a neighborhood theater that wasn't quite as spiffy as the Empire, but it was running *The Cat and the Canary* with Bob Hope and Paulette Goddard, along with something called *Television Spy* as the second feature. I was really looking forward to the Hope picture. You know how I love comedy and horror all mixed together.

But we never got there.

Of course, there were short subjects before the first feature, including a cartoon that had that kid "Scrappy" in it. It was mostly about a hobo who thought he was inheriting a million bucks but instead inherited a million _cats_, and Dianna seemed to enjoy it like a child would, squeezing my arm and smiling when the bum put on airs. She laughed out loud when he got his inheritance and the felines jumped all over him.

Then came the newsreel. And John, honestly, I'm not sure what happened, or why. One minute, we were watching it together, my arm around the back on the seat – and then, all of a sudden, I felt her begin to tremble. When I looked over at her, I saw that she'd turned away from the screen as though in terror, with big, wet tears streaking her face. Of course, I took her right out of the theater. When the doors below the lighted marquee closed behind us, she burst out into wracking sobs, and I held her close as we made it to her auto.

Inside, we sat for a while, as she slowly got herself together. I didn't say anything, mostly because I didn't know what to say.

Finally, she managed to say, "Horrible." She shook her head, wiping at her tears. "Horrible."

I thought back to the last thing we'd seen on the screen. It was, I remembered, newsreel footage of a fox hunt in England. The dogs had overtaken the fox, and while the camera had discreetly pulled away from the carnage, it was clear that the animal had been ripped to pieces.

"The fox hunt?" I asked.

She only nodded, sniffling.

"That's what upset you?"

She nodded again. "It's horrible. Barbaric." I handed her a handkerchief, and she wiped at her face with it. "Why would people _do_ something like that?"

"I don't know, Dianna. I really don't. But I sometimes hunt."

She gasped. "Foxes?"

I shook my head. "No, no. I don't go on fox hunts. But I hunt squirrels and rabbits and birds – ducks and pheasant. And I always eat what I shoot."

Oddly enough, she seemed relieved. "That is permissible," she said, "when you eat what you kill. It's the natural way. But murdering little living beings that you don't eat and have done you no harm – I don't understand that." Taking a deep breath, she continued. "I'm afraid I have ruined your evening. My apologies."

"Nonsense," I returned. "How could it be ruined when you're a part of it?"

Then she did something else I didn't expect. She grabbed me and smashed her lips against mine with a ferocity that surprised me. We were parked right there on a side street, with several store windows lit up with their Christmas displays, people walking by, and it didn't seem to make a damned bit of difference to her.

I was stunned and of course pushed her away. Ha – you know better. And there we were, suddenly petting hot and heavy right on an avenue in Washington, D.C. Wowzer! I won't say much else, except for a couple of things: No. 1, whatever "tutoring" she got must've included a sex manual, and No. 2, if a cop had come by, he could've arrested us and made it stick. Thankfully, the street remained cop-free, and the people passing didn't pay us any attention. They seemed a lot more interested in the window displays along the sidewalk.

I was still in a kind of fog when I drove back to the boarding house and got out of the car. She planted one last powerful kiss on me and asked, "Tomorrow?"

As I nodded and started to say "you bet!" I heard a sudden

high-pitched barking behind me. It was the dog I told you about earlier, the one that lives in the alley behind the boarding house. He was really going to town, whining and growling and yapping, leaning toward the car threateningly, eyes wide. I couldn't figure out why. From my point of view, he was a pretty easy-going mutt.

Then I saw Dianna, folded up against the seat behind the steering wheel, her face frozen with fear. "Take him away, Robert!" she shouted. "Make him stop!"

I turned to the dog, concentrating, remembering what the Destruidoras had taught me back in Arkansas. And suddenly, it worked! I was seeing the scene through the dog's eyes, as though I were looking into the view-finder of a camera, everything in black and white – including Dianna, huddled there in the driver's seat of the Nash. But _not_ Dianna.

It's hard to explain, John, but through the eyes of that mutt, I saw her as, well, as a kind of sparking and snapping ball of energy, with two flashing eyes in the middle. My seventh sense suddenly rose like floodwaters. And I was barking _with_ the dog, or so it seemed – I felt what _he_ felt, blood-rage, and I knew he was going to attack her and I had to stop him. I was outside him, but I was _in_ him, too. Hell, I _was_ him! And I had to stop him, or myself, from attacking this young woman!

It's crazy (and maybe even funny) to say this, but all I could think about was not letting our date end like this, with a girl I liked a lot mauled by a dog who'd let me see things through his eyes.

I look back on that sentence, and how looney-tunes it sounds, but that's exactly what was going through my head. It was like I was putting the brakes on a speeding truck, or pulling the reins on a runaway stagecoach in a western movie, trying with all my mental power to keep the mutt away from her. It all played out in the space behind his eyes, as I kept willing him, hard and continually, to pull back. (I have no idea what my actual body was doing at this time, although dimly I thought I heard myself talking quietly. To the dog? To Dianna?) It was a tug-of-war, a struggle, and it wasn't helped by the vision of Dianna as some black-and-white pulsating wraith from out of the ether.

The front door of the Nash suddenly slammed in front of me, or us, and the spell was broken. Like a shower of falling stars in the night sky, the vision faded as Dianna drove away, maybe a little faster than normal, and I was back in my own body, standing beside the now-quieted mongrel from our alley, who looked up at me as if to say, "What in the hell was *that* about?"

I wish I'd had an answer for him.

We stood there for quite a little while, watching until I couldn't see Dianna's auto any more, Finally, the dog trotted off behind the boarding house and I started up the steps of the porch. I couldn't believe no one had heard the melee out there until I realized that, except for the barking of the dog, it had mostly played out inside his skull, where he and I had it out over Dianna.

Suddenly, I felt the familiar fluttering of the two-cent piece against my chest. I looked around in the darkness but didn't see anyone or anything but the familiar wooden facade of the boarding house, the dim light inside the living room. It was maybe a minute or two before the witch-charm slowed to a stop. And about that time, behind my building, I thought I heard the sound of a door closing – the door of Mr. Saki's garage apartment.

Your harried pal and faithful comrade,

Robert

December 16, 1939
Sunday afternoon

DEAR JOHN,

It's afternoon now. I finally slept – right through Mrs. Dean's Sunday lunch spread, which is usually pretty good because it's hard, even for her, to foul up cold cuts. So I'm hungry, but I'll eat something a little later on, after I get this and my previous missive in a stamped envelope for you. I'm going out soon and I'll put it in a mailbox so it can go out tomorrow.

This one will be quick. I just wanted to tell you that the only reason I'm up now is that one of my fellow tenants – a beanpole named Clyde who works at the Treasury Department – banged on my door a few minutes ago to tell me I had a 'phone call. (I think Clyde has been, as the saying goes, "unlucky in love"; he seems to be the boarder who uses and hangs around the telephone the most, and from the tenor of his conversations, he's not talking to his dear old mother.)

Anyway, I threw on some clothes and padded downstairs, still a little fuzzy and worn-out after the events of last night. I'd like to say I was surprised to find Dianna on the other end of the line, but something – sure, you know what it was – told me that's the voice I'd hear when I picked up the receiver Clyde was holding out for me from the wall 'phone.

"Are you all right?" she asked without preamble, after I'd said hello.

"Sure," I returned. "You?"

"I want to apologize. I left you without saying goodbye. It was impolite."

"Maybe, Dianna. But under the circumstances, justified. No apology's necessary."

"There's something else. Something I must ask you. It's been bothering me since I left you last night."

"Go ahead," I said.

"Are you . . . magic?"

I looked around. Clyde was plopped down in the big over-stuffed couch in the living room, right next to Mrs. Dean's slightly raggedy-looking Christmas tree, a few dozen yards across the floral-carpeted floor from me. He appeared to be reading a western pulp, and Mrs. Dean herself was bustling around back in the kitchen, but I still knew they had their antennae up. This was hardly a conversational topic I wanted to get into with potential eavesdroppers so near.

"That's a little complicated," I said. "If you'd like to come over, we can go somewhere and talk about it."

"I'll be there in an hour."

"All right," I told her. "See you then."

Clyde looked up at the click of the receiver, and I nodded my thanks at him and headed upstairs to change into some decent clothes and get this letter written, trying to think of just what the hell I was going to tell her and why she'd asked in the first place. This time, there was no whirring of my two-cent piece, but my seventh sense was definitely astir, giving me the feeling that my association with Dianna Jones was headed to a new level.

When I find out exactly where that level is, you'll be the first to know. Or maybe the second – after Dianna.

Your pal and faithful correspondent,

Robert

December 18, 1939,
Monday evening

DEAR JOHN,

I'm telling you, there's something about Dianna Jones that I just can't figure out, something odd. You know my seventh sense seldom lets me down, but around this gal all it does is give me an off-kilter feeling. I don't know how much of that is mixed up with my feelings for her, which have been growing stronger and stronger. Could she be the one to make old Robert settle down in a house with a picket fence? I don't know. She doesn't seem the picket-fence type.

But that's enough of that. I don't want you getting this letter mixed up with a first-person tale in *Love Story* magazine.

So here's the latest on us. Exactly an hour after I'd hung up the boarding-house phone, Dianna's Nash pulled up in front and she slid over to let me drive – but not before planting a big kiss square on my lips. I kind of hoped some of my fellow roomers were spying on me.

I drove us out to Anacostia Park, which you may remember as the place where all those Bonus Army guys congregated a few years ago, before MacArthur ran 'em off with his infantry and cavalry. Not long after that, the National Park Service took it over, and it's nicely maintained, mostly brown now with winter on us. When we got there, it wasn't crowded at all. We pulled under a big old tree and I cut the engine.

"All right, Dianna," I said, aware that my seventh sense was bubbling through me, and also aware that I was close to forgetting about having any conversation with this beautiful young woman in favor of another petting party. Something in her guileless brown eyes, though, told me I'd better keep my masculine instincts in check.

"I'll repeat what I asked you on the telephone, Robert. Are you magic?"

"I'm not sure what you mean."

"Last night," she said. "When that dog came at me. I was

terrified. It was about to spring and tear out my throat – I know it!" She took a breath, calming herself. "And then, as I looked into its eyes – I saw _you_, holding it back."

"Well, sure, Dianna," I said. "I was right beside –"

"I don't mean you held it back with your hands," she said quickly. "I mean you held it back from inside its own head. I saw you looking out of its eyes!"

Well, John, I wasn't at all sure what to tell her. Of course, I could've denied it, but I've never been a very good liar – especially when it comes to women I really like (even if there haven't been that many). So I shrugged, trying to act like it wasn't any big deal.

"Sometimes, I guess, I can do things," I said.

"Magic things?"

"Yeah."

"Can you show me?"

"Dianna, magic is nothing to fool around with."

"I know. But it's . . . _important_ that I know."

As I let that statement sink in, my seventh sense heightened, letting me know that I needed to listen to this woman, and not only that. I needed to show her some magic. I got the sense that it was indeed important – for both of us – although I had no clue _why_.

I exhaled, knowing that I'd better follow my intuition.

"Yes," I said. "Yes I can."

She clapped her hands together like a little girl. "When?" she asked, beaming.

In a flash, I thought about what I needed to do, the things I had to get.

"Give me a couple of days," I said. "How about Tuesday? We'll have to do it in my room and be very quiet about it; if Mrs. Dean catches us, there'll be Old Ned to pay. You cannot make any noise."

She smiled at that. "Robert, you needn't worry. I can move like a shadow. I promise you that no one else will hear a thing."

"Okay. Then Tuesday night I will give you a glimpse of the future through magic. But remember, we can't do much talking. No conversations. Mrs. Dean's walls are thin as her porridge."

The smile stayed on her face, even as she leaned in to me. "Sometimes," she whispered, "actions are better than words."

Indeed.

Your pal and faithful comrade,

Robert

December 20, 1939,
Wednesday morning, 2:15 a.m.

DEAR JOHN,

I have had one hell of a night. One *hell* of a night. I don't understand all of it, but I'm hoping that by getting it down on paper I can somehow exorcise the conflicting feelings that have been ripping me apart ever since Dianna left. The Blue Norther rattling the windows doesn't do anything for my mental state, either, but I guess it was good to have wind and noise to help cover her trip to my room. I'd hate to be out in the elements right now, but that's where I'd probably be if Mrs. Dean had caught us.

At nine o'clock, I met her at a prearranged spot a couple of blocks away. With the wind howling around us and the hard snow pelting our faces, we made our way to my rooming house, making sure not to get out in the open anywhere that Mr. Saki might be able to spot us from his garage apartment window. I didn't figure he'd be out in the elements, and I hoped I was right. My seventh sense told me it was important that he didn't know about what we were doing.

Dianna was right – she could glide like a shadow. Twice, I had to turn to make sure she was still with me. When I did, her eyes almost glowed back at me, and she smiled with those perfect teeth, whiter than the snow that swirled around us. When we got to the back stairs, I pointed to the outside edges, indicating the parts of the steps that would make the least noise. Nodding her understanding, she joined me, and in no time at all we were in front of my room. Quickly, I keyed the door, hustling her inside, and before I could reach the light switch she grabbed me and kissed me hard. That shot my blood pressure up, but business is business, so I pulled free and went to the windows, making sure all shades were completely down.

Dianna looked around and sniffed the air, and I realized that it was the first time she'd ever been in my room. I figured she was sniffing because there were some interesting smells in the air – the Yuletide scent of holly, and the astringent, minty aroma of hyssop. With Christmas only a few days away, the holly had been easy to find, but I'd had to go to several stores before I found any hyssop.

To the undiscerning eye – say, Mrs. Dean's – it would just look like I'd decorated for the season. But I knew from my books on the occult that the leaves of both those plants provided good insulation against witchcraft, forming a barrier that makes it hard for anyone to spy on you via magic. Since the witch-charm I wore had told me Mr. Saki had some of those sorts of powers, I figured it would be prudent to construct that barrier, just in case.

Holding a finger to my lips, I switched on the light and nodded toward the floor, where I had pulled back my rug to reveal a pentagram on the polished wood and set out candles and little salt dishes of water at all the prescribed positions. I had left a gap in the pentagram for her to cross, a gateway to the center.

Gesturing for her to stand in front of it, I got down on one knee and touched my Ronson to the first candle. The flame immediately jumped up with a height and brightness that surprised me. So did the others. The flaring lights seemed to kindle my seventh sense, but it was certainly too late to turn back now, so, with another hand gesture, I indicated that Dianna should now step into the pentagram. Once she was in, I entered behind her and once again went to the floor, picking up the piece of chalk, completing the symbols for my "prediction spell," and then closing the pentagram with one long stroke.

Suddenly, the candles flared up even higher than before and there was a loud blast of escaping air, like someone had opened a giant coffee can. It startled me, and I turned to Dianna.

She was gone.

I've got to stop for a minute now. I have a huge case of the heebie-jeebies.

- -
- - - - -

I don't know if I'll be able to finish this or not. It's taken a couple of shots of Mr. Boston's brandy to calm my nerves, and now it's after 3 a.m. and I've got work tomorrow, plus I'm feeling the liquor – so we'll see and here we go.

I stood there stunned, racking my mind for a rational explanation. The pentagram and artifacts were supposed to screen anyone from outside magic, and so was the holly and hyssop, so she couldn't have been whisked away by Mr. Saki or any other magician. Then, what in the name of all that's holy had happened?

When I heard the tiny frightened yelp at my feet, the answer hit like a thunderbolt. Nothing "holy" had happened. Looking up at me was a small red fox, its large brown eyes uncannily mirroring Diana's.

The truth of it slammed me so hard that I felt myself wobbling, like I'd been hit with one of those roundhouse rights I took back in my CCC days. But I was able to keep the presence of mind to erase a part of the pentagram with my foot, knocking over a water dish in the process.

Again, a hissing blast of air, blending with the whistling noise of the raging snowstorm outside. And Dianna stood beside me, as naked as the day she was born.

"Dianna," I whispered, taking her by the shoulders. "Thank God you're all right."

She started to say something, but broke instead into hysterical sobs. Quickly, I led her through the gap in the pentagram to my bed and sat her down. Even in the midst of all this, I admit I had a fleeting appreciation of how good she looked in the raw. It took some effort to block further carnal thoughts, but I did, scooping up her clothing from the now-opened pentagram and whispering, "Quiet. Shhhh. You're okay. But you can't be discovered here. We have to be quiet – remember? Put on your clothes. Quickly, now."

With some effort, she smothered her sobs down to a soft hiccupping and began dressing. Much as I would've liked to have watched that process, I turned away, my mind racing. I knew now what my seventh sense had been trying to tell me about Dianna and her "otherness." She was a were-creature, a fox transformed into a human by occult means, created for some undoubtedly sinister purpose. They always were. My seventh sense reinforced that conclusion, even as stories from arcane tomes rushed through my mind – tales of were-animals, controlled by their creators, sent out to do unholy work.

But this wasn't just some *creature*. This was Dianna Jones, a woman – I *thought* – who had begun to capture my heart, as B-movie melodramatic as that sounds.

Was she a woman? *Was she?*

Her touch on my shoulder actually made me jump.

"Now you know," she whispered as I turned. Tears still welled in her luminous eyes, her face was wet and red, and all I could think was: *This girl – this beautiful girl I might be in love with – isn't human.* Yet, when she reached for me, I didn't hesitate to embrace her.

"Mr. Saki," she whispered. "He can't see us?"

"No."

"He controls me, you know. I am very afraid of him. If he finds out you know about – about me, he will destroy me."

I continued to hold her, saying nothing.

"When I saw you in that dog's eyes, I knew you were magic. Now, you and your magic – you have to save me. I know you can. Please." She sobbed again against my shoulder.

Suddenly, I was thankful that my witch-charm wasn't moving, even if my seventh sense was echoing through me like a fire alarm. At least Mr. Saki wasn't around.

I pulled her away from me, holding her by the shoulders, and looked as deeply as I could into her eyes. "Dianna, you are a were-animal, aren't you?"

She nodded, sniffling.

I didn't want to say the next thing, but I had to. And when I did, the words almost hissed out of me. "I know about were-animals. They're people created to do animal things. To kill."

She began to sob again, but I had to get it out.

"Am _I_ one of the people you're supposed to kill?"

She gasped at that, and the look of horror on her face seemed genuine.

"Oh, _no_," she whispered. "How could you even think that? You are my teacher, and teachers are sacred. You were to teach me how young people act in this place and time, which would make it easier when the time came for my . . . tasks."

"This have something to do with the war?"

She turned her head down, nodding. I took a deep breath.

"All right," I said. "All right."

John, it was all just a little too much. It seemed like every time I used magic, there was some sort of backlash. This time, it had shown me that this woman wasn't a woman at all, not really. She was an _animal_. That was still sinking in as I began picking up the candles and water dishes, erasing the chalk-marked pentagram with my shoe. I really didn't know what to say next.

Even though I was conscious about the importance of not making any noise, I guess I was snatching the stuff up pretty aggressively, because she asked me if I was angry with her. I looked up, shaking my head. "No, Dianna, not with you," I said. "Just with the situation."

She stepped to me and touched me gently. "That can change. You are a magic man, and you can _make_ things change. I am so unhappy. But you can save me. Take the spell away. I'll be happy to live in the forest again. Or . . ."

I looked up as she paused. Slowly, the agony on her face softened. She even smiled a little. "Turn me into a human being – for all time. I love being human. And I love being around _you_."

So many emotions – major- and minor-keyed, indescribable – along with the seventh sense crashed through me then, like waves in an oceanic storm. I turned away from her, wiping with my foot at the last vestiges of chalk marks left on the floor, and heard myself mutter, "Hell, why not?" It was just a murmur, but she _did_ have the ears of a fox. So she heard me.

She dropped to the floor then, putting her head against my shoes and looking up at me with unalloyed hope. "Oh, if only you could," she said. "It would be heaven to me. I could never thank you enough." She gripped my ankles hard, her eyes wet and glowing.

"Okay," I said. "But please get up now. Of course, I'll do everything I can to help you."

Honestly, John, I didn't know if that was the right thing to say or do. I knew now she was a tool of Mr. Saki and God knows who else, created to do harm right here in our nation's capital. Maybe I'd always known that Mr. Saki was a lot more than just a "house boy"; his mysterious benefactor – that "American friend" – who'd supplied me with all that cash to take Dianna out, was likely getting his orders, and the money I'd taken, from the Japanese government itself.

Then there was this: Even if I turned Dianna into a full-time woman, there was no assurance that she wouldn't continue on the course that had been planned for her by her overseers. But when I looked over and saw her, eyes averted, I was filled with some sort of mixture of – I don't know, love and pity, I guess, and something even bigger. I guess you could call it a sense of _rightness_, of doing something that was bigger than just me and what _I_ wanted. Strange as it seems, for the first time in this whole damn month, I felt the stirrings of what everyone calls the Christmas spirit. I understood in that moment that the distilled essence of Christmas is doing something for someone else. A simple message. A profound one.

"All right, Dianna," I said. "This season is a time of

powerful goodwill for people of my --" I paused as she looked up at me" – _faith_." Damned if I hadn't almost said "species."

"So, on Christmas Eve, I will do my best to not only remove your spell; I'll try to turn you into a human being for the rest of your natural life."

She let out a small yip of joy and was on me then, kissing and hugging me until I could calm her again. "Now listen, Dianna," I told her softly. "As is the case with all magic – mine, anyway – there are no guarantees. I _think_ I can do it, but I'm not 100 percent sure."

Her grip on me slackened, and the fear returned to her eyes.

Quickly, I added, "In my studies, I've run across an ancient spell that changed a were-wolf into human form and kept him there. They had a different objective then, of course." I didn't tell her the objective was to destroy the wolf creature forever. "I think this would work on you."

I looked at my watch. Only an hour or so had passed since she and I had entered my room. It seemed an eternity.

"We've got to go now," I told her. "C'mon." I wasn't crazy about getting out in that knife-edged wind and pelting snow again, but I hustled her up and we both headed back the way we'd come, thankfully running into no one either in or out of the house. I thought that given the still-raging Blue Norther, maybe I ought to drive her back to her home – wherever that is – but she kissed me, said she'd be fine, and took off after we made our date for the night of the 23rd, which will extend into Christmas Eve morning. That's when I'll try to break the spell and let her live the rest of her life in human form.

And if you think that's a lot to digest in one letter, all I can say, brother, is that you should have lived it.

Your pal and faithful comrade, full of beans or hope (not sure which),

Robert

December 22, 1939
Friday evening

DEAR JOHN,

We had a Christmas party today at the office, and while there was plenty of revelry, food, and even some champagne (which Mr. Fletcher seemed to enjoy plenty of, even though he never really acted like it affected him), I laid off the booze and left a little early, as I was still searching for that damn spell. I wandered down through the streets toward my trolley stop, passing storefronts all lit up with elaborate displays. Although my mind was focused hard on the spell and what was coming up, I found myself standing in front of a jewelry-store window, where a toy train wove in and out of a papier mache mountain, around little mechanical puppets of the Seven Dwarfs, moving their mining tools up and down. Each train car emerged from the mountain with something different in it – a watch, or a necklace, or a ring, all shiny and glittering. I don't know how long I stood there, lost in the scene, before I roused myself and headed for the stop. Even the trolley cars are lit up with Christmas lights now.

Work has seemed dreamlike and unreal ever since what happened Tuesday night with Dianna. I'm still trying to come to terms with how I feel, knowing now that she's not really a human being. Or maybe she is. Or will be, once I try the spell.

Which leads me back around to the search. I have three big boxes of books on the occult here in my closet; the same ones I had back in Arkansas. I was sure the were-animal spell was in one of them, but I couldn't remember which one.

I thought it might be in *The Book of Black Magic,* which is the rarest book on the occult I own, having been privately printed back in 1898. So I went through it page by page but came up with big zeroes. Then, I remembered *Human Animals*, that 1912 volume I'd used before, back in Arkansas. And sure enough, there it was right in the text: the spell for transforming a were-animal back to a human being.

I've got lots to do tomorrow before picking up Dianna. I need to gather up the necessary "articles," memorize the basic spell, and go back to *The Book of Black Magic* again to incorporate some other things into the ritual. I've even got to find a white, 100 percent linen shirt from Ireland, which the *Human Animals* book says I must have for the spell to work. If there's any place in town that would have something like that, it'd be Hy's, and I'll bet it's going to set me back a pretty penny (even with my "employee's discount").

Still, in for a dime, in for a dollar. I've been going over the White Magic that worked for me back in my Mackaville days, and combining it with the blacker stuff from the two books, I should have a winning formula. Or maybe I should say I *hope* I have a winning formula.

We shall see. I'll fill you in later on all my preparations.

Your pal and faithful comrade,

Robert, the amateur warlock

December 23, 1939
Saturday morning

DEAR JOHN,

I've been up early, working on the spell. In fact, I've got it memorized now, letter-perfect, but it's such a mixture of White and Black Magic that I honestly don't know if it'll work. It'll be almost 24 hours before I can find out, and I'm not sure what I'm going to do with myself for all of that time. I could try to read a pulp – I've got several of 'em stacked up – but I want to be able to keep my focus on the upcoming task as much as I can.

Not that I'm likely to forget about it for even a second.

Good old Hiram Gold did have the shirt called for in the book. It's a little big for me, but I got it this morning anyway – for 50 iron men! He spent a long time explaining just how expensive Irish linen was and how only rich people wore it and how sorry he was he couldn't give me more of a discount, etc. But I hardly heard him. I was just glad to have it. It wasn't until I was out of his store with the package that I realized the whole thing would've had to be called off, or at least postponed, if Mr. Gold hadn't come through.

Maybe Someone Up There is looking out for me.

I'd found a store in the telephone book that sold items for Catholic Churches, so I took the streetcar to a part of town I hadn't been to before and bought some large, fat beeswax candles and vials of holy oil and water, deflecting questions about my "church" from the overeager old-lady clerk. The final stop was a department store, where I bought a nice box of expensive bath salts and powders and had it gift-wrapped.

When I got off the Christmas-lit trolley in front of the boarding house an hour or so ago, Mrs. Dean was standing out on the porch, looking up at the sky. Since the storm Tuesday night, it had been cold but bright, but I saw now that big dark clouds had begun to roll in, stacking up against one another in the sky.

In a moment, she looked down and saw me, so I knew I couldn't duck her. I just hoped she wouldn't be too nosy about my armload of purchases.

"Mr. Brown," she said as I drew near. "Been Christmas shopping?"

I stopped, shifting the packages until I found the one I wanted.

"Yes, ma'am," I said. "In fact, I have one for you." Walking up onto the porch, I handed her the gift-wrapped bath stuff.

John, you should have seen her eyes as she held it up, examining it from every angle.

"Well, thank you, young man," she said, giving me a smile that I don't think I'd ever seen on her face before. "That's very thoughtful. I'll put it under our tree and open it on Christmas Eve." Then, she nodded toward the sky. "Hope you're staying in tonight. Paper says another big snowstorm's on the way."

"I'm going out for a while, but I'll be back," I said as I elbowed open the door and slipped in. "Merry Christmas, Mrs. Dean."

"Merry Christmas, Mr. Brown."

The living room was deserted as I made my way toward the back stairs, thinking how a little kindness goes a long way. That exchange was probably the longest conversation I'd ever had with my landlady – and certainly the best.

I'm going to pull back the rug and start chalking the diagram now. The next time you hear from me, you'll know whether all of this worked or not – and so will I.

Your pal and faithful comrade,

Robert, the would-be warlock

December 24, 1939
Sunday, Christmas Eve
4:33 in the afternoon

DEAR JOHN,

I've been asleep for nearly ten hours, and I still feel like a man in a dream. But I want to get all the details down on paper before they flitter away like so many moths. If I wait too much longer, if I don't write you until I've rejoined the world and had some human contact, I'm afraid my perspective will shift and I won't remember what I need to remember about last night and this morning.

So here goes.

First, I should tell you that I caught a break yesterday afternoon. I was down in the dining room, wrestling with a ham sandwich, when Mr. Saki came through. I have suddenly become Mrs. Dean's fair-haired boy – thanks, I know, to the Christmas package I gave her – and she was hovering over me like a mother hen. The only other boarder partaking of her cold cuts was a little chubby fellow named James "Buster" Keaton who also works as a government clerk/typist, but in a different building than mine. He's a good man, very easygoing, but when Mrs. Dean wasn't looking he rolled his eyes at me, wondering why I suddenly warranted her attention.

When she went off to the kitchen with Mr. Saki, Buster grinned at me. "Looks like you're in good with the old battle-axe," he whispered. "How'd you do it?"

"Just my personal magnetism," I said. "And a Christmas gift." I nodded toward the tree in the next room, my package propped up right at its base.

We were interrupted when she and Mr. Saki walked past us. They were still talking, and the gist of their conversation seemed to be about his taking Christmas Eve off. I felt that Mrs. Dean and I were such good chums now that I could inquire about her business, so when she returned – without the old man – I asked if Mr. Saki was leaving.

"Yes, he won't be back until Christmas Day," she said. "Some sort of doings at the Japanese Embassy. A big party, he says, and he'd like to stay overnight. I guess even heathens celebrate the birth of our Lord."

I wouldn't have put it quite that way, but it was a break for me, anyway. Still, I decided to leave the hyssop and holly up in my room, just for good measure.

A few hours later, I was piloting Dianna's Nash Ambassador to the Golden Eagle, which had become "our" restaurant. Things seemed a little strained at first. She was beautiful, as usual, and I can't deny how I've felt about her, and how it was building. But knowing – well, knowing what I know about her, I understand that everything has to be different now. It's one of the oddest, most unsettling, damn feelings I've ever had.

At the Golden Eagle, where we had our usual fare and she made her usual visit to the Christmas tree at the end of the bar, we got into a discussion about religion, something we've never really talked about before. Given her . . . origins, I guess it's not surprising that Dianna is pantheistic, believing that God is everything and everything is God. This was especially true, she said, of things from nature – and suddenly, I understood why she was so attracted to that little tree. I figured she maybe saw what the ancient Druids and the others saw in evergreen branches –- eternal life, protection against negative forces, the hand of the Creator.

I told her I felt almost the same way she did about God, except that I thought He was *in* everything rather than *being* everything. This distinction provided plenty of fodder for our suppertime conversation, which was a good thing, I think, because it occupied our minds and kept us from reflecting too much about the darker things on tap for later. Or from considering the fact that I now knew she wasn't, and could never be, fully human.

I'd intended on taking her to a movie, but once we were back in her automobile, she told me she'd like to go dancing. She knew of a little nightclub not far from the Golden Eagle, so we headed there. By the time we arrived, snow had begun to fall.

It was warm inside, and not crowded, with a good Negro combo laying down the rhythm. It was the first time we'd ever danced together, and she was wonderful to hold, very graceful. I found myself wondering if that grace was human or feline.

At a little after 11 p.m., there were only two other couples on the floor, and a guy who looked like the manager came out in front of the band and said the next song would be the last for the evening, as he was letting the musicians go home for Christmas. We danced to that tune – a languid but jazzy version of "My Reverie" – and then we left, with the combo going into an impromptu "Jingle Bells" behind us.

Out on the street, the snow had gotten thicker, with wind beginning to whip it up. Still, we drove around for a while, because I had this feeling, without anything, really, to support it, that performing the ritual on Christmas Eve was important. I was still getting surges of "Christmas spirit"; maybe that had something to do with my timing.

When I reminded her about the "powerful goodwill" of Christmas Eve and Christmas, she snuggled closer and said, "I trust you, Robert. I am in your hands."

Although I knew Mr. Saki was gone, and the snowstorm was becoming stronger by the minute, I still found a parking place a couple of blocks away, hoping our luck would hold and we could sneak in undetected again. If I got caught with a girl in my room – and never mind with a floor full of magic symbols – I don't think all the bath salts in the world would have kept Mrs. Dean from pitching me out on my ear.

Once again, the winter tempest covered our entry, and we were upstairs and in my room in what seemed like a flash. Motioning for her to be silent, I changed into the Irish linen shirt, drew back the rug, and placed the beeswax candles in their proper places on the diagram, which I'd painstakingly copied from *The Book of Black Magic*. Like the pentagram of a few nights ago, it had an unchalked place to enter, but I'd also drawn a big box, which had its own entry point, around it. Outside of it, I'd marked a big white "X" on the floor.

By this time, it was hard to tell what was raging more – the snowstorm outside or the seventh sense roiling inside me. Turning to Dianna, I kept my voice as calm as I could.

"Now," I said, "you have to get this exactly right, and that means you have to be completely natural. No clothes."

She nodded, and as she undressed I stepped into the diagram. When she was standing in the altogether before me, I nodded to the vials of blessed oil and water atop my chest of drawers.

"Take those," I told her, "and move to the ` X. ` I'm going to start speaking the spell, and once I do I can't stop until it's all concluded, so when I point to you, pour the contents of both those bottles over your head."

She nodded again. For the first time, I could see that she was trembling. Suddenly, I felt sorry for her. She had to be scared to death.

It was time.

I had determined not to call upon Satan or any of the other demons commonly summoned through Black Magic, but instead to invoke the names of older "gods," a couple of which had been around thousands of years before Christ. My assumption was that they would recognize the power of the Old Testament Yahweh and therefore be willing to help with the spell.

"Now we begin," I said. And taking a deep breath, I started the chant, remembering to keep my voice down.

"I exorcise thee, Vulpes vulpes, in the name of Jesus Christ, who came into this world for the salvation of both the guilty and the innocent. I conjure to remove the spell immediately from this creature, the innocent victim of malicious magic. I conjure thee without the circle, accursed one! Begone Vulpes vulpes – begone without any deceit whatever and leave a beautiful and well-favored human form of soul and body. I do this in the name of the God of gods and Lord of lords: *Adonay, Tetragrammaton, Jehova, Otheos, Athanatod, Ischyros, Sady, Cados!"*

My voice was rising. I willed it to come back down.

"I call upon Bymon, most potent king, who reignest in the West. And Amoymon, most potent king, who reignest in the north. Come forth and render aid! I call and invoke thee in the name of the one true God that thy must recognize! Help me to break forever the spell upon this woman!"

At those words, a window-rattling wind slammed against the building, and I swore I heard thunder, John – *thunder*, in a snowstorm! I pointed to Dianna then, and as she poured the contents of the vials over her head, a nimbus of green light flashed around her. An unintentional wail escaped from her lips, but she silenced herself as I shook my head at her and continued chanting.

As I watched, the soft light surrounding her grew brighter, going from green to blue. Winds howled outside and a lightning bolt flashed, followed by an enormous peal of thunder.

"By penitence already, and by the pure innocence of her soul, she has earned the right of freedom from her curse," I continued, aware of still another lightning flash. "I exorcise thee, Vulpes vulpes, the Fox, forever in the ineffable name of God! Go forth. Go forth!"

Again, I pointed at her. A flash of pure white light sprang from my index finger to her chest. She let out a muffled scream then – and all the candles, the light around her, everything, went suddenly dark as the inside of a tomb.

Then, another lightning flash illuminated the scene, and for just a moment, she and I were statues, frozen in the blackness. The west wind shook the west side of my room, the north wind shook the north side, lightning struck again – and then, complete silence. Even the wind stopped.

I glanced toward the window. The snow fell lightly now, whispering down from the sky, welcoming in Christmas Eve, 1939.

It was beautiful, and I stood transfixed for a few moments, grateful for the sudden calm. Then I reached across and snicked on my desk lamp. In its soft yellow glow, I saw Diana, still shaking, unharmed – but *different*, somehow. There'd been a subtle change in the coloration of her skin, but, more than that, there was the distinct impression that *something* had gone out of her, had risen and evaporated, just like the oil and water she'd poured over herself that had, inexplicably, left no traces.

Stepping across the now-powerless diagram, I looked into her eyes, realizing that both my seventh sense and my witch-charm were still and quiet.

"Merry Christmas, Dianna," I said softly. "You are now a human being."

A laugh that was almost a sigh escaped her lips, and she fell into my arms for an embrace that expressed nothing but pure joy. I laughed a little then, too.

"Get dressed," I whispered. "We've got to be leaving. I'll get this stuff picked up, just in case my landlady decides to get nosy while we're out."

Gathering up all the articles as quickly as I could, I stowed them in my bottom dresser drawer under the extra shirts and then began eradicating all the chalk marks with a rag. When I was finished, I turned – and Dianna was gone. Only her pile of clothes was left.

Panic flashed through me. Then, a soft whisper of my name took it all away.

I turned to see her, smiling, stretched out under the blankets on my bed, beckoning me.

"Before we go," she said. "Come over here. I will give you your Christmas present now."

Your pal and faithful comrade,

Robert

P.S. No, John, I can't leave it there. It's not fair to you.

I didn't . . . take advantage of Dianna's offer. You know from what I've told you before that working magic takes enormous psychological and physical effort. Frankly, I was just too fagged out. I could've fallen asleep right there. I almost did.

And then, there was the fact of her – what? – her nonhumanness? She's a human now, and will be until the end of her life, if that spell is what it was made out to be. But my knowing what she was, or what she had _been_, would always have been a wedge between us.

Here's something funny. When I stopped typing this letter for a moment, I heard muffled voices from downstairs, singing "Away in A Manger." They're not very good, but there seem to be several, including a wobbly soprano that has to belong to Mrs. Dean. I'm sure they're down there around the tree, smiling as they warble those old carols; suddenly, I have an overwhelming urge to join 'em.

So I'll sign off, after I tell you that Dianna is gone. She left after I told her thank you and Merry Christmas again and kissed her, but only once. She seemed to understand why I had to pass on the tryst she offered, leaving like a silent shadow.

It's that O. Henry Christmas story, isn't it? I gave her what she wanted most, and she wanted to give me, in return, the thing she thought would make me the happiest. It just didn't quite work out the way either party thought it would.

My seventh sense is telling me I'll never see her again.

The voices downstairs have now segued into an approximation of "I Heard the Bells on Christmas Day." They put me in mind of cats on fences, but for some reason, on this snowy Christmas Eve night, they also sound like a celestial choir.

God bless us, everyone.

CHAPTER 4
SEVENTEEN DAYS OF DECEMBER
BY KENNETH ANDRUS

TARGET SUPERSTORE
COLLEGE STATION, TEXAS
WEDNESDAY 8 DECEMBER

"Nick Parkos. What a surprise."

Nick's hand tightened around the box of Christmas tree lights he'd selected, his hummed song of "The Little Drummer Boy" jarred to a halt by the familiar voice. He turned to confront the FBI Agent who'd positioned himself on the other side of the shopping cart. "Vanatsky."

"None other," Gunnar Vanatsky replied, a sardonic grin crossing his face.

"What the hell are you doing here?"

"Shopping."

"Bull—" He dropped the rest of his expletive as a young mother and her daughter passed by. "You just happen to be in College Station almost fifteen-hundred miles from D.C., and bump into me at Target?"

"I take it, you don't believe in coincidences."

"The last time I saw you, you'd slapped handcuffs on me and dragged me out of my office accusing me of treason."

"Yeah, that was unfortunate."

"Unfortunate? You damn near cost me my job." He swung his head through an arc looking for Vanatsky's partner who'd be lurking nearby. "What are you doing here?"

Vanatsky cast a furtive look at a young man who appeared at the head of the aisle. "I'm investigating a scientist who may have ties to the Chinese Ministry of State Security. Jessica said you might be able to provide an assist. By the way, she said to pass on her regards to you and Michelle."

Assist? Michelle? He dropped the Christmas lights into the cart, struggling to maintain his composure. First Vanatsky appears out of nowhere, and now the guy just dropped the name of his wife in the same sentence as his friend, Senior Special Agent Jessica Caudry. "You keep my wife out of whatever-the-hell you're up to."

"We have no intention of involving her."

"What are you not involving her in?"

"We're cleaning up a few loose ends from the Lin-Wu operation."

"We wrapped that up last year."

"Your part anyway."

That statement aroused his curiosity. "What's going on?"

"We identified a scientist named Derek Yang who's working for the Chinese. I suspected he was working on something Covid related, but things didn't add up."

"Never heard of him."

"I'd be surprised if you had. He's been hired by a new startup in College Station, Company called, AmpTex. The Bureau—"

"That's it." He grasped the cart's handle, spinning it

around on its front casters. He had no intention of getting pulled into Vanatsky's web of intrigue. "We're done. I've got to finish shopping."

"You know, we indicted that professor from Cal Berkley."

Nick spun to face Vanatsky. "Hopkins?"

"Yeah, turns out he was..." Vanatsky paused. "This isn't the place. We'll talk later."

"What makes you think I want to talk to you?"

Vanatsky gave a wry shake of his head and started to make for the exit. "That's what Geoff told me you'd say. We'll be in touch."

NICK WATCHED Vanatsky until he and his partner disappeared, stunned at the mention of his close friend, Geoffrey Lange. Geoff was the head of The Curators, a deep, clandestine unit of the National Security Agency. Geoff, as-well-as the Director of the National Security Agency, Bryce Gilmore, also knew he wanted to take a break after their last op in Prague. But more to the point, why was Geoff even involved with Vanatsky? *What-the-hell is going on*? "Damn."

His eyes darted to another parent and child hoping they hadn't heard his expletive. They didn't react, so he turned his attention back to shopping. He looked at the crushed box of Christmas lights in his cart, grabbed another off the shelf just to be safe, then made his way toward the shelves of Christmas ornaments.

"May I help you, sir?"

He looked up at a young, red-shirted woman with a Santa hat perched on her head. "Oh, I think I'm on the right track. I'm looking for ornaments."

"It can be a bit overwhelming. Can I make some suggestions?"

Busted. "That'd be great."

"For starters, how big is your tree?"

"Ah..."

"Do you live in an apartment?"

"The Station. I want to surprise my wife. We got married in June."

A bright smile greeted this statement. "Well, congratulations. That's a good place to begin."

Ten minutes later, his cart was full of various sized blue, silver and gold ornaments and several bunches of matching garlands. An angel wasn't necessary. Michelle had the one that had topped her family's tree since she'd been a child. Her mom had insisted. Her mom was cool that way. He studied his purchases while weaving his cart through the crowded aisles toward the checkout counters, the store's overhead speakers playing, "All I Want For Christmas."

A small, carved, wooden Christmas tree to his right caught his eye, pulling a memory of another past operation from his mind. The twentieth of December. Neum, Bosnia-Herzegovina. The al-Khultyer affair. He'd been watching a man carve a traditional Georgian Christmas tree, a *Chichilaki*, from a thick branch of walnut. He smiled at the recollection. While exquisite, the finished piece of art, topped with a black ribbon, reminded him of a Yeti you might see in a Muppet movie.

He pulled is hand back from the shelf, resisting the temptation to buy the tree. He couldn't let his new life with Michelle be defined by his past but, at that prompt, an idea popped into his head. A gift that had earned him major points when they were dating, a bone carving of a great white snowy owl. He turned on his heel and went back to the ornaments. *There it is.* The large white owl was close enough to Harry

Potter's 'Hedwig the Owl' he'd bought for her while on a mission to Alaska. *Perfect.* He grabbed the ornament and headed back to checkout, his encounter with Vanatsky pushed from his mind.

~

THE STATION APARTMENTS
COLLEGE STATION, TEXAS
WEDNESDAY 8 DECEMBER

NICK SET down two of the largest Target bags, fished out his key, unlocked his apartment, and pushed open the door. He was greeted by his adopted stray, Bill the Cat, who'd been lying in wait near the entryway. He'd named his pet after the frazzled feline in the Opus and Bloom County cartoons and he'd made a great companion. Bill brushed up against his leg, emitting loud purrs now that his food source had returned.

Bill was huge, a good twenty pounds, and always hungry. Nick reached down and gave his pet a vigorous scratch behind his ears, then picked up his bags and deposited them in the hall closet. "Sorry, buddy. No treats, but Michelle should be home soon." With that, he headed back to his car to collect the Christmas tree stand. He wanted nothing to do with an artificial tree, that, and they didn't have room to store one anyway.

His balanced the stand on the back wall of the front closet hoping it wouldn't fall if Michelle happened to open the door. He paused then plucked his perfect ornament out of the top bag not wanting Michelle to see it or have it broken. He studied his gift, trying to decide whether to wrap it or place it on the tree Christmas Eve so she'd spot it in the morning. His decision was deferred when his iPhone sang out Aerosmith's "Dream On." He glanced at the caller ID. Michelle. "Hi, there."

"Hi there, yourself. I'm stopping by Antonio's to pick up a pizza. Pepperoni with extra cheese. I'll be home soon."

"How'd you know I had a pizza craving?"

"You always have a pizza craving and the mouse likes getting into the refrigerator when he gets hungry in the middle of the night."

"Not."

"I also got some cookies from our class party."

"Yumm. Hurry home. I'll pour a couple glasses of the Merlot."

He started for the kitchen when he heard the rumble of a truck pulling up outside. He reversed direction hoping it was the American Girl doll they'd ordered for his daughter. Michelle declared that Emma was old enough, eight, and it would be a great gift. They'd settled on the Camille doll and some of her accessories after browsing through the catalog Michelle had gotten from a friend. Finding something for his ex, Marty, had been a bit tougher, but Michelle knew exactly what she'd like.

Marty had moved to Miami after their divorce to be closer to her parents and a new job. Their parting had been amicable enough, both acknowledging the difficulty of adjusting to the responsibilities of adulthood after their carefree days at Ohio State. They went their separate ways, but remained friends. Marty had even sent a really thoughtful wedding present. He only wished he could spend more time with his daughter.

His thoughts drifted to the colorful, spotted unicorn that Emma had named Mr. Sprinkles. He'd bought the gift for Valentine's Day just days before that crazy home-grown terrorist ... He suppressed the rest of the memories, opened the box and studied "Camille." She even looked a bit like Emma and the accessories--including a mermaid tail that could be slid over the doll's legs and a pet seahorse--were fantastic. Wow, major points for Michelle.

"Hey, Camille arrived," Michelle noticed as she closed the front door. Bill followed her and the pizza box into the kitchen, tail held expectantly in the air. "Hold on there, buddy." She set the pizza box on the dinette table, then scooped up their feline, gave him a good rub on the head, and headed back to examine the doll.

"She's great," he said. "Figure we can wrap the rest of the presents tonight if you're not too tired. They should all fit in the flat rate box I picked up yesterday."

"I'm never too tired for Christmas," Michelle replied. Her eyes lit on the accessories scattered on the floor.

"Sorry, I got distracted. No wine."

"No kidding. Should I buy you one to play with?"

"Only if you're going to be gone for a long time."

"Nope, I'm not going anywhere, but my last day of classes was today. I gotta spend a little time going over my notes for the Newtonian Mechanics exam this Friday." She planted a kiss on his cheek. "How was your day? You get any more research done on your grandparents' keepsake box?"

Nick had found the ancient wooden keepsake box with a faded white lion on the top in his grandparents' attic. A distant cousin in Prague, Petr Hájek, who had been the focus of his last operation, possessed the key that opened the box, literally unlocking his family's past. "Not much. I went shopping." He didn't mention his encounter with Vanatsky.

The other piece that factored in that decision was how important her classes at A&M's school of Aerospace Engineering were to her—to both of them. A prior enlisted member of the flight crew for Air Force One, she aspired to fly F-35 stealth fighter jets and the Air Force was paying for her education including a cost-of-living stipend under the Airman

Scholarship Program. When she graduated, she be commissioned as a second lieutenant and, if all went well, she'd go to pre-flight school.

Her green eyes sparkled at his revelation. "Ooh, let me see. Let me see."

"Nope. Secret." He returned Camille to her box and stood. "How 'bout settling for a hug?"

"After you pour me some wine and we have our pizza."

No further prompting was required and he headed for the kitchen, exhaling a sigh of relief. Michelle had an uncanny ability to read his moods and she hadn't picked up on the undercurrents of foreboding that racked his mind. *If that damn Vanatsky screws up our first Christmas....*

～

THE NICHOLAS
3136 M STREET NW
GEORGETOWN, WASHINGTON D.C.
THURSDAY 9 DECEMBER

GEOFFREY LANGE RESTED his Ashton ESG cigar in the ashtray and studied the flames dancing in the fireplace of The Nicholas' upstairs drawing room. Fire, flames were an apt analogy considering the conversation he had a couple hours ago with Bryce Gilmore, the Director of National Intelligence. Gilmore wasn't pleased with how the FBI was handling the operations in Texas. He wanted the traitor, Yang, in jail before Christmas. The soft buzz of his secure iPhone that linked to the caller with end-to-end encryption prompted him to pick up the device. He expected the call and slid the answer bar. "I wondered how long it'd take you to call. How you doing?"

"At the moment," Nick replied, "I'm not a very happy camper."

"I can't say that I didn't warn him. And, no, before you ask, I didn't tell him where to find you." He took a pull of his cigar and blew out a plume of silver-white smoke. "By the way, where did he find you?"

"The Target store. I was shopping for Christmas ornaments."

"The Grinch who stole Christmas?"

"Pretty much."

"What'd he want?"

"He didn't talk to you?" Nick asked.

"For less than a minute. He wanted to know where to find you. Something about tying up some loose ends from the Lin-Wu op. Mentioned that they'd indicted that professor from Cal Berkley, Ron Hopkins, and were investigating some bioengineer whose name they found on a list of compromised academics in Lin Wu's place. He then dropped yours and Jessica's names without providing specifics."

"What did you tell him?"

"That if he found you, you'd tell him to pound sand."

"That pretty much sums up what I said."

He chuckled and raised an eyebrow at Edmund MacDonald who had appeared with a refresher for his Lagavulin scotch. Ostensibly The Nicholas' doorman, he was, in fact, ex-British Special Air Service and another member of his team. "Can't say I didn't warn him. What did he have to say about Jessica?"

"Only that she passed along her regards."

"That's it?"

"Said, 'We'd talk later.'"

"Persistent son-of-a-gun." He decided to hold back on everything he knew and judge Nick's reaction. "My take is he's on to something. He happen to mention someone named Derek Yang?"

"Matter of fact he did. I told Vanatsky I wanted nothing to do with whatever-the-hell he was up to."

"Remember the note I sent to you on your computer?"

"How can I forget. "It's Not Over.""

"Appears things with our friends in Beijing aren't. Vanatsky implied there's a connection with that Yang guy and some company in College Station, a bioengineering firm named AmpTex. Hold on a sec, let me double check the name." He grabbed his iPad from the side table and did a search. "Got it. There's another company with a name similar to it, so when you look it up, don't confuse them."

"Don't bother. Vanatsky mentioned the place. You presumed I looked it up."

"You did. Bill's not the only curious cat in your household."

"Harumph."

He nodded to Edmund who, in turn, gave an amused shake of his head. *Game on.* "That comment's exactly what I expected. Hold on, I've got something. Let me drop a couple of abbreviations on you from their webpage: CRISPR-Cas9 and iPSC. I'm not sure about CRISPR, but iPSC is short for 'induced Pluripotent Stem Cells.'"

"Isn't a crisper something you put your lettuce in?"

He ignored the quip and focused on what he'd found. "Here we are, CRISPR: 'Clusters of Regularly Interspaced Short Palindromic Repeats ...'" His voice trailed off. "Man, I've gotta get a lot smarter."

"I sure-as-hell don't have a clue," Nick added.

He did another search after Edmund gave a negative shrug. "They look to pertain to genome sequencing."

"Covid?" Nick asked.

"I'm thinking something else. If the Chinese were responsible for the virus, they'd be smart enough to bury anything that pertains. There's enough flack floating around with the Wuhan lab and NIH grants."

"Could there be a link to that Hopkins guy Vanatsky mentioned?"

"Wasn't Hopkins involved in something else entirely?"

"Yeah, you're right," Nick said. "Maybe the link is Beijing's program to penetrate an academic's research."

"How 'bout you start working on one of your Venn diagrams?" Before he'd left, Nick had been known within the Agency for the use of this simple analytic tool that enabled him to connect disparate clues to a common element. He thought of him as a bit of a savant.

"Wonder if Vanatsky can access the names of AmpTex's employees?" Nick asked. "If so, Austin can match them against the files he created for Beijing's United Front Work Department and their Student and School Association. He also has access to the data bases I created for the other Americans the Chinese may have corrupted with certain inducements."

He studied the glowing tip of his cigar. *Good thought.* Austin Mack had been Nick's assistant and moved up to take his spot when Nick had left the Agency. "Grants—"

"Yeah, and other stuff," Nick added.

"You want to call him?"

"No, it'd be best if you do. Keep things in house now that I'm out."

The way things were shaping up, he knew he had to get down to College Station. "Speaking of house. You up for a guest?"

"Sure. You want share a cushion with Bill?"

"Just kidding. So far, I'm just bringing Edmund. We'll find a place. And doesn't Michelle have finals coming up?"

"Tomorrow. Newtonian Mechanics."

"Good Lord. We'll be sure to stay out of her hair. I'll check in tomorrow if I have anything new." He terminated the call and addressed Edmund. "Things are about to get complicated."

"Ach, are we about to entangle our reluctant hero in another escapade?"

"I'm not sure I'm left with any other choice. We need his brain."

"You gonna take a trip to see Vanatsky?"

"Yeah. We gotta stop Yang before there's any chance he disappears with his research. I want this op wrapped up before Christmas."

"Could be tricky with the jurisdiction issues."

Lange looked at his watch. "I've got an appointment to see the boss in an hour. He told me he's already spoken with the AG."

"I'll work the aircraft," Edmund said.

CASTLEGATE II HOMES
2018 WESTVIEW COURT
COLLEGE STATION, TEXAS
FRIDAY 10 DECEMBER

DEREK YANG, former tenured professor in genetics at Harvard University and one-time Army researcher at Fort Detrick, leaned back in his high-backed leather chair pondering the implications of the coded message he'd received a minute ago. The solitude of his home study in the upscale subdivision of Castlegate II provided the ideal place to pursue his secret life. He closed the worn code booked disguised as a copy of

Southern Living, dismissing the warning from his handler. His intellect was superior to any supposed threat.

His few friends in College Station would have never guessed the critical role he played in facilitating China's goal of seeking world dominance. His work with the Chinese was well masked but, none-the-less, there were a few hints that suggested that he might be more than the mid-level genetics researcher at the new startup company, AmpTex, that he professed to be.

An aging forty-two years of age, of average height, he styled his coal-black hair in an authoritative side part, equal in length on top and the sides. In the same vein, he also chose to wear contact lenses, succumbing to this bit of vanity. His clothing reflected his futile attempts to counter his tendency toward chubbiness, choosing to lessen this flaw by his selection of well-tailored, but modest, clothes. With those considerations, his physical attributes and quiet demeanor masked an incredible intellect. His IQ of 158 qualified him as a genius.

His genius went hand-in-hand with his narcissism, a flaw by its very nature he couldn't acknowledge, and a defect that contributed in large part to his dismissal from his previous places of employment. His transformation had been insidious, driven by forces he didn't recognize, but forces that others in the Chinese Ministry of State Security understood and used to manipulate him.

Both Harvard's and the Army's programs were also loosely affiliated with the Department of Bioengineering at Texas A&M, and those relationships, in turn, accounted for two things. The subtle overtures by Beijing and the subsequent deposits of large sums of money in a Swiss account. He held no qualms about accepting either or the opportunity to further his research at AmpTex unfettered by government oversight.

He lived modestly, the exceptions being his home and his

indulgence in a metallic-blue Tesla Roadster. His eyes came to rest on a model of his car on the bookshelf to his right. Capable of a top end speed of 250 mph, he raced along the empty country roads of west Texas and had driven the roadster to the small town of Sanderson to roar along U.S. highway 285 in a sponsored event sanctioned by the State Highway Patrol.

"Are you going to spend all morning in your office?"

He glanced up at the young woman leaning languidly against the doorframe, her long, honey-blonde hair topped by a red and green elf hat. The enticing curves of her body, high-lighted by her sheer negligee, stirred his manhood. Another of Beijing's inducements. Santa's helper.

"All work and no play?" she asked in a seductive, smokey tone.

He set aside his musings at the sound of her voice and the enticing bouquet of cardamon and mimosa from the Jo Malone perfume he'd bought the young woman.

She ran a feather duster she'd dangled in her hand across her breasts. "Perhaps you would care to assist me with my housecleaning?"

He stood and followed her to his bedroom, any further thoughts of his research or incipient danger tucked away in the dark recesses of his mind.

∽

FOUR POINTS SHERATON
COLLEGE STATION, TEXAS
SATURDAY 11 DECEMBER

GEOFF LANGE SET ASIDE his irritation at having lost a day, but Vanatsky had provided a plausible excuse for not being able to meet with them yesterday. He and Edmund had taken advantage of the open time to conduct surveillance and acquaint themselves with the lay of the land.

He leaned forward in the bucket armchair that had been pushed in the corner of the cramped room. "I'm presuming you have something on Yang. Otherwise, you wouldn't be down here."

Vanatsky closed his laptop and swiveled the desk chair to face him. "I do and, to be clear, my team is operating under the umbrella of the Justice Department's China Initiative. Our reporting senior is the Associate Attorney General for National Security. And before you ask, the AG has already spoken to Director Gilmore to define the specific roles of our respective agencies in this investigation."

A start, but this was hardly an investigation. The DNI had briefed him on the fledgling operation before he'd left Washington and the clock was ticking. He suppressed a smile recalling his *brief.* He refocused. The China Initiative was an extension of the president's national security policy that also drove the NSA's Cybersecurity and Infrastructure Security Agency's (CISA) actions against Chinese State-sponsored activities and, by extension, the clandestine operations of The Curators. Gilmore had made it clear in no uncertain terms that The Curators would take an aggressive role in the FBI's operation.

He decided to address the underlying issue. Their respective agencies' deeper interests in the operation were unlikely to align. "And Yang?"

"He showed up on the list of possible compromised academics we found in Lin-Wu's home. Their Global Experts 1000 Talents Plan."

Lange understood the implications of the 1000 Talents Plan, the link to the United Front Work Student Department, and the Student and School Association. He'd have to touch base with Austin Mack, Nick's former associate, to see what else they could glean from their previous operation pertaining to Beijing's programs. "You have anything hard?"

"We got him making a probable dead drop."

"Who picked up the material?"

"A Chinese national we've tied to their Ministry of State Security. We suspect the package may be SD cards."

"I'd think passing Secure Digitized information to a MSS agent would be enough to make an arrest. That's a clear felony."

"The Assistant AG wants an airtight case before we move. And he wants to take down AmpTex."

He wasn't convinced AmpTex was complicit. "What about the honey-blonde?"

"How'd you know about her?"

"A little bird whispered in my ear."

Vanatsky's right hand clenched, then relaxed. "She's pretty much an unknown. Nothing on facial recognition, but we tracked her to a small apartment across town. My—"

A knock on the door cut the agent off and prompted Lange to stand. "Company." He crossed the room and admitted Nick.

"Well, I'll be damned," Vanatsky said. "I thought you didn't want to talk to me."

"I don't." Nick gestured to Lange. "I want to talk to him."

Lange shook his head. "Well, I'm gratified to see you two have hit it off so well." He turned to Vanatsky. "You were saying?"

Vanatsky appeared to swallow a retort and picked up where he'd left off. "My guys are checking it out. Right now, we don't have enough to obtain a warrant to search her place or bring her in."

Lange cast a sideways glace at Edmond who had propped himself up on a couple pillows of the room's king-size bed and appeared to be watching the evening traffic on George Bush Drive. He mouthed the name of another team member. *George.* Edmond returned his look with a subtle nod.

He'd likely regret the decision he was about to make, but then again it wouldn't be the first nor probably the last. There wasn't time to screw around. They would conduct their own black bag operation and George was their expert in surreptitious entry. He addressed Vanatsky's other statement. "The company's leadership, or the folks at A&M for that matter, may not even know what's going on. I'd move on Yang before it's too late."

"I happen to agree with you about the other people who may, or may not be involved. That said, my boss and the AG believe we have time."

"Perhaps, but our friends in Beijing are operating under no illusions or timelines. They're playing hardball and may know we're on to them."

Vanatsky's face flushed with anger. "Are you saying we have a mole?"

He held up his hand. "No. I'm operating on the premise they're on to us."

"Better safe than sorry."

"Exactly."

"What do you have planned?"

"It's best you don't know."

Vanatsky swung his chair to face Nick. "Are you in?"

"It appears I'm about to be," Nick replied.

98 EL LARGO ROAD
BRAZOS COUNTY, TEXAS
SUNDAY 12 DECEMBER

"Vanatsky is totally off base," Lange said. "My read is he's an aggressive agent when it comes to taking down a bad guy, but there's a disconnect. Makes me wonder what other factors are in play."

Edmund poured a generous glass of a blended Scotch whisky from a distillery he didn't recognize and handed it to George who had flown in a few hours before. "Careful of the enamel on your teeth, mate. This stuff may take it right off."

The product offended Edmund's sensibilities, a selection that he described in his tasting notes as akin to wet leather. He'd bought the product at a local package store situated near the western border of Brazos County. The store, a block from their safe house, was in a neighborhood that would be well out of sight of the prying eyes of any Chinese operatives who might be lurking about. He dropped down on the living room couch. "That's my read. Has he dropped any hints?"

George took a sip of the whisky, grimaced, and addressed Lange's observation about Vanatsky. "Agreed, but something else must be going on." He downed the remainder of his scotch. "This isn't the time to be playing by the rules."

"With the way things seem to be playing out, it'd be best not to involve Nick," Edmond added.

Lange hefted his glass, acknowledging the third and last member of his team. He took a contemplative sip of his drink and reached for a cigar from the box he'd brought from their aircraft. "Agreed. The Chinese have likely identified all the local FBI assets and we have to assume Nick's been tagged."

"And Michelle," Edmond said. "Lin-Wu said she'd be harmed if Nick didn't cooperate. He must have communicated her identity and relationship to his superiors before we took down his operation."

He slid off the wrapper of the Cuban Cohiba Siglo cigar and clipped off the tip. "Nick's already involved."

Edmond cast an interrogative eyebrow.

"I didn't ask him about Michelle."

"Knowing him," George said, "he won't sit on the sidelines. His antipathy towards the Chinese knows no bounds."

Lange struck a wooden match, holding it above the tip of the cigar while rotating it to ensure all parts of the root were evenly heated. Satisfied, he took a deep draw while studying the tip to ensure it burned evenly. He whipped out the flame with a flick of his wrist. "Nick's on board. I'll place a call to the DNI to get his read. In the meantime, we should stand up the rest of the team."

"Same folks as the Prague operation? Vinny, Ann, Jennifer, Tom?" Edmund asked. "Vinny can run counter-surveillance. Jennifer and Ann can run interference and keep tabs on our blonde. Tom can apply a bit of muscle if needed." He paused. "You want to bring in Jessica?"

"No, not right now. It's best we don't place her in the middle trying to choose sides between us and the FBI."

"Makes sense," Edmund admitted. "That'd also make penetrating the AmpTex building less tricky."

"That's off the table. Security's too tight. That and our timeline is too short fused to put together a workable plan."

"How about we place a call to our Israeli friends?" George asked. "Have them run a cyber-worm like their Stuxnet that took down the Iranians' uranium centrifuges."

"That'd be ideal, but again we're up against a timeline. They couldn't develop the lines of code needed to weaponize and insert their malware. That's even taking into account we don't know what kind of lab equipment Yang's been using." He took a long draw of his cigar. "I wants this op wrapped up before Christmas."

"Getting sentimental on us?" George asked.

"I have my moments," he replied, electing not to share what incentivized him.

Edmund topped off Lange's glass, nose crinkling in disapproval.

"What's the matter?" Lange asked.

"It offends my sensibilities to pour even something as plebian as this offering into a plastic bathroom glass."

"Ah, the sacrifices we must make for God and country." He lifted his glass in acknowledgement. "Cheers."

THE STATION APARTMENTS
COLLEGE STATION, TEXAS
MONDAY 13 DECEMBER

NICK STUCK his head into their kitchen, prompted by an incredible aroma emanating from the oven. All of the available counterspace was covered. Bowls, measuring cups, their new Kitchen Aid mixer, bottles of Brer Rabbit molasses, spices, rolling pin, all covered with a fine dusting of flour. "What on earth are you doing?"

"Making ginger bread men," Michelle answered with a wave of a dough covered spatula. "It's a family tradition. I made the first batch of dough last night after you went to bed."

"Good, grief. How many are you making?"

"Maybe ten dozen." She pointed to a slip of paper on the dinette table. "See if I missed anyone?"

He swiped his finger along the Kitchen Aid's mixing paddle as Michelle made her way to the refrigerator to rearrange the contents and make room for another bowl of dough. "Yumm. Is there anything I can do besides get in the way?"

"Well, you are pretty good at that, but you could go to the

grocery and pick up some more cinnamon and ginger... and another Teflon baking sheet. It's a win, win. You're out of my hair in this tiny kitchen and you're doing something useful."

"On my way."

"Oh, and some vanilla for—"

The doorbell rang, cutting off whatever else she was going to say. "Are you expecting anyone?"

"Might be FedEx. I'll get it." He opened the door. *Not FedEx.* Edmund, attired in the traditional highland kilt, socks, vest and jacket of the MacDonald clan, held up a bulging brown shopping bag. *"Nollarg Chridheil."* He made his way past the astonished Nick followed closely on his heels by Geoff and George.

"Ah...?"

"Wow," Geoff exclaimed. "What's that great smell?"

"That's Michelle's gingerbread," Nick managed to answer.

"Aye, and tis a wonderful smell at that," Edmund said while beckoning Michelle. "How 'bout a *smourich*, lassie?"

She gave him a hug and a kiss on the cheek. "How can I resist, you handsome devil."

"Ah, a devil I may be and that I should have such a lassie." He stepped back and pulled out a lump of coal. *"Lang mae yer lum reek.* I had the devil's own time finding this and I don't see a fireplace."

"Reek?" Nick asked.

Michelle grabbed her mystified husband's hand. "Gaelic. 'May there always be a fire burning in your hearth.' The coal is for our fireplace."

"We don't have a fireplace."

"Details."

Absent a fireplace, Edmund made for the kitchen, trailed by a curious Michelle. "May I use your table, darlin?" He proceeded to empty the rest of his bag on what space remained on the dinette table. A quart jar of a milkish looking slurry, a small bottle of honey, a pint of cream and lastly, a bottle of Aberfeldy 12 year scotch Whisky.

"Oooh, you're going to make *Atholl Brose.*"

Nick peered over her shoulder. "You know what he's doing?"

"Of course. It's a traditional holiday drink. Remember, my family's roots are Scotch-Irish. Jacobites. The McClungs were scattered after Bonnie Prince Charlie was defeated at the Battle of Culloden. Some made their way to the colonies." She began to sing:

"Sing me a song of a lass that is gone. Say, could that lass be I? Merry of soul she sailed on a day, over the sea to Skye."

The men stood transfixed. George found his voice first. "I didn't know you could sing. That's beautiful."

She cast a knowing look at Edmund and gave her red hair a toss, her green eyes sparkling. "Aye, we Scots have a lot of secrets."

"Ah, tis true. Tis true," he replied. "Now, shall we make this brew?"

∽

AMPTEX HEADQUARTERS
COLLEGE STATION, TEXAS
TUESDAY 14 DECEMBER

THE VISUAL IMPACT of AmpTex's campus that Yang had first seen seventeen months before never diminished. The futuristic design of the three-story central building with its cantilevered windows topped by an elevated, flat overhanging roof was a statement to the work being done inside. The glass panels were twenty-four feet high and made of a material that reflected back different colors based on the viewer's perspective. The facilities exceeded even his expectations as did the largesse bestowed upon him by his benefactors.

He strode across the inner courtyard with its cascading waterfall and made his way to his office, his thoughts focused on his work, his mind devoid of any suggestion of the upcoming holiday. He powered up his computer and accessed his encrypted data bases, the software platforms and bioinformatic programs that he'd developed for the specific gene editing sequences that targeted two major components—the Cas9 nuclease and their companion guideRNA (gRNA) sequences. Working with these, he'd developed a purified plasmid complex to target the DNA region matched by the gRNA carrying Cas9. In turn, he'd been able to cleave a specific region of double stranded DNA to assemble a new Cas9 and gRNA construct.

Few, if any, at AmpTex could fathom what he'd done, but to ensure nobody stumbled across his breakthrough, he shrouded his work under the guise of applying his research to the study of a new toxic mold destroying Asia's rice crops, threating the region's food supply.

He'd discovered the keys to his ground-breaking research during his time at Harvard, understanding that his work in human augmentation concepts could also be applied to brain science, artificial intelligence, and supercomputing. Frustrated by the ethical barriers thrown in his way by his well-meaning, but naive, co-workers, he went in search of a sponsor to further his work. Like his new sponsor, he could not be unencumbered by ethical boundaries in his pursuit of power and fame.

He held no doubts that his name would be recorded in history beside—even exceeding—the greats of his profession. Watson and Crick, Ledeberg, Dobzhanky, but primarily? Charpenter and Doude, who'd been awarded the Noble Prize for their discovery of the CRISPR/Cas9 genetic scissors that formed the foundation of his own research.

Movement beyond the glass enclosure of his workspace caught his eye. He suppressed a frown at a co-worker stringing Christmas lights at her workstation. There would be no distractions. He'd speak to her later for he had no use for Christmas, the myth of Santa Claus dispelled in his youth by his father.

His cynicism also extended to religion for he also had no use for mythology, Marx's "Opiate for the masses." He paused. Like so many things, the quote, part of Marx unfinished *A Contribution to the Critique of Hegel's Philosophy*, had been taken out of context. No matter. He considered Marx to be a secular humanist. And opium? The drug relieved physical and emotional pain as did the masses' belief in obscure deities. Despite these assessments, he had no use for religion...or any sense of moral obligation to society. Only his work mattered.

He selected an expresso coffee pod from several varieties he kept in his desk drawer, inserted it in the Nespresso machine next to his computer, and spun his chair to face his workbench. Next to his computer was the Xcell Electrophoresis System and a florescent cell imager. He down-loaded his latest program into the Xcell machine. Only 60x30x45 centimeters, the machine was the heart of his next generation DNA sequencing experiments. Such a small device that would enable him to change the world, gifting humanity and his benefactors with unheard of capabilities. His goal was no less than the creation of the first super-human.

～

THE NICHOLAS

3138 M STREET, NW
GEORGETOWN, WASHINGTON, D.C.

THURSDAY 16 DECEMBER

ANN BALEK AND JENNIFER MYSEK, still using their *noms de guerre*, were seated in the paired wing-back chairs facing the fireplace of the drawing room of The Nicholas. They were on their second sturdy gin and tonic, comparing notes on what they had planned for Christmas before they'd received their summons. They paused when Marie Lynne appeared at the top of the stairs carrying a large cardboard box.

Marie set her box down on the room's ornate writing desk, grabbed a matching chair from in front of the library's bookcase, and set it besides Ann's. "No food pairings?"

"We've been left to our own devices since Edmund's not around." Jennifer peered over Marie's shoulder. "What's in the box?"

"Christmas decorations. Thought we'd surprise the crew. Vinny should be here in a bit with more stuff."

"Sure beats what we were doing," Ann said.

"And that would be?"

"Dwelling on the implications of CRISPR/Cas9 genome editing and the current research on iPSC induced unipotential stem cells."

"Good, Lord. Is that what this is all about?"

"Geoff's told us Vanatsky's got evidence that some wacko might be trying to develop a super-human. All hypothetical, but Geoff's been talking with Nick about running a sanity check on Vanatsky's hypothesis."

"Ah, oh. That's trouble," Marie said.

"What? A super-human or Nick?" Ann replied with a chuckle.

"Both," Jennifer replied.

"Yup," Marie agreed. "We hoped Michelle would be able to keep her new husband in the box."

"Not if she's fallen under Edmund's spell."

Jennifer polished off her drink and stirred the fire. "I'd say it's the other way around."

Ann pointed to a bucket of ice, a plate of sliced limes, Fever-Tree tonic, and a bottle of Brookers London Dry gin she'd grabbed from the first floor bar. "Here, make yourself a drink. I'm thinking you'll be needing one."

"Or two." Marie dropped a couple ice cubes into a cut-crystal glass, poured a healthy double shot of gin, topping her drink with tonic and a squeeze of lime. "Is Jessica joining us?"

"Geoff thought it best not to get her involved," Ann replied. "He's got something in the offing and doesn't want to place her in the middle of what he's got planned and Vanatsky's guys."

"Oh, boy."

"Close," Jennifer said.

"The target have a name?" Marie asked.

"Derek Yang."

Marie shrugged. "Doesn't ring a bell."

"Some obscure genetic researcher supposedly working for the Chinese. Vanatsky got wind of him when he was cleaning up the loose ends of the Win-Lu op," Ann said. "The AG sent Vanatsky and a team to College Station to check out a new startup biotechnology company named AmpTex who'd recruited Yang. The trip-wire for the op was the background check on Yang after his name was on a list of academics Beijing had ensnared."

"What does the company say?"

"He's supposedly doing cutting edge research on a toxic mold infecting Southeast Asian rice crops."

"You believe them?"

"Not a chance in hell."

Jennifer filled in the blanks. "The DIA and our folks at the NSA have evidence to suggest the Chinese are already conducting human testing. They're attributing their findings to reports they received from India's National Security Council concerning the Chinese army's actions along the Sino-Indian border. Our analysts initially attributed the NSC's reports to the PLA's use of exo-skeleton suits, but subsequent reviews by researchers at Lockheed Martin who've seen the videos and who are developing an Exosuit for the U.S. military say Chinese soldiers were carrying 'super-human' loads only partially accountable for by the use of exo-skeletons."

"So, what's in store for us?" Marie asked.

"Geoff's targeting a honey blonde woman who's been frequenting Yang's home. Wants us to provide an assist."

Marie looked at her box. "Guess we'll have to put the decorating on hold."

"Geoff's sending the Gulfstream for us," Ann said. "We're going to bring our lady in for a little chat while George cases her apartment."

"Sounds like a plan," Marie said. "When do we leave?"

Ann checked her watch. "We gotta be at Executive Aviation in four hours."

~

98 EL LARGO RD
BRAZOS COUNTY, TEXAS
FRIDAY 17 DECEMBER

GEOFF LANGE SURVEYED his team crowded around him in the safe house's small living room. Vanatsky leaned against the far wall, arms crossed. "I have confirmation from our CISA folks."

He then proceeded to outline what the NSA-supported

Cybersecurity and Infrastructure Security Agency had developed in what they'd named their MITRE D3FEND program. A framework defining a sequence of cybersecurity countermeasures: Harden, Detect, Isolate, Deceive, Evict to identify and neutralize malicious activity mapped by their MITRE ATT&CK's reconnaissance program.

His eyes settled on the FBI agent after he'd finished. "I don't think we have any other viable option but to conduct a snatch."

Vanatsky's face flushed. "I'm not going to permit a bunch of damn cowboys undercutting my operation." He placed his right thumb and first finger an inch apart. "We're this close to nailing that bastard and I've got the tools, the legal tools. The Foreign Agents Registration Act and the Foreign Investment Risk Review Modernization Act."

He listened calmly letting Vanatsky say his piece while choosing to ignore the agent's use of '*my operation.*' "Considering we're in Texas, cowboys might not be a bad analogy, but I'm thinking the Texas Rangers are more apropos within the context of our current situation."

"You're not grabbing Yang."

"We don't have any intention of doing so. We want the girlfriend."

Vanatsky uncrossed his arms. "To what purpose?"

"We just want to have a little chat." He aimed his chin at George. "while George here takes a look around her apartment."

"That's against the law."

"We don't plan to abduct her."

"You don't have a warrant," Vanatsky countered.

"We figure you can get the FISA approval from the Federal Surveillance Court after we provide you the supporting justification."

"That's ass backwards." Vanatsky shot a withering look at Lange, then George. "There's no way in hell you're entering that apartment without a warrant."

"Agreed, but absent anything firm on Yang, we need to flip the girl."

Marie chose that moment to intervene. "Gunnar. Ann, Jennifer, and I can do the heavy lifting. Figure we girls can just have a little talk. Get her to do something that spooks Yang and forces his hand."

"I may have enough to get our warrant," Vanatsky admitted. "Give me another day."

"Care to share what that is?" Lange asked.

"No."

"You have something on AmpTex?"

"And a professor at A&M. Another name from Li-Wu's file."

"Lying on a Federal Grant application?"

"Yeah. We've got Yang lying on a grant application and the illegal use of U.S. grant funds to develop scientific expertise for China, conspiring to steal trade secrets—"

"Enough to disrupt the operation," Lange said. "All right. We'll give you your day and keep things nice and legal while turning up the heat."

Vanatsky held out his hand. "Agreed."

PARK PLACE APARTENTS
COLLEGE STATION, TEXAS
SATURDAY 17 DECEMBER

"Think that's her real hair color?" Ann asked, slowing her pace as they approached the Park Place apartments. The three-story brown and tan clapboard affordable units, set along a park bordering the shores of the Brazos river, were mostly inhabited by A&M students...and their mark.

"Maybe. But you don't see many real honey-blondes," Jennifer said. She pointed to a flaming red Kia Sorento. "I'm still wondering about her car. Expensive. Wild color, too."

"I think it's called Passion Red," Marie added.

"Appropriate, don't you think?" Jennifer observed.

"Too bad she has a flat," Ann said.

"She doesn't look real happy with our work," Marie said. "Time for the good Samaritans."

Marie completed a quick scan of the street and didn't see anything suspicious. She wished Vinny Cade hadn't been pulled for another detail. She trusted his eyes. She caught up with the others as they stopped by the Kia.

"Bummer, that's a really flat tire," Ann said. "Need some help?"

The honey blonde twisted to face the newcomers. "Oh. Yes, I sure could. Thank you. I've gotta get to work."

Marie crouched down to examine the left front tire. "Nail." She pointed to her two friends. "We've had plenty of these. Can you pop the trunk? We'll put on the spare. It'll last until you can get to a gas station."

Ann walked to the back of the car at the sound of the latch release. "Damn, the spare doesn't look good. Can we give you a lift somewhere?"

Their mark bunched her eyebrows in thought, then brightened. "That'd be great. My name's Amanda."

Marie made a quick decision. "I'm Zoe." She gestured to Ann standing by the trunk. "That's Sam."

"And I'm Britany," Jennifer said. "Our car's just down the block."

A few minutes later, Ann took a left-hand turn to head

west. She didn't have to wait for Amanda to respond as their panicked passenger gripped the door handle.

"This isn't the way."

"Yeah, we know," Marie replied to the sound of the automatic door locks. "We— rather you, have another problem."

"What's that?"

"Derek Yang."

Amanda starred at her captors. "But ...."

Ann pulled over and stopped at the curb. "Yang will never know you talked to us. If you cooperate, we'll go back, change your tire, and let you go."

～

CASTLEGATE II HOMES
2018 WESTVIEW COURT
COLLEGE STATION, TEXAS
SUNDAY 18 DECEMBER

MICHELLE PULLED her eyes from the beautiful homes dotting the large lots of Castlegate II. "Do you have any idea why Geoff asked us to take a Christmas tour of this neighborhood? I mean, it's nice and all, but it's not even dark and we can't see the lights."

"I know about as much as you do," Nick replied. "He was pretty vague, but wants us to drive by this house on Westview and check it out. I'm thinking it may belong to the person they're looking for."

"Vague isn't like him," she replied, second guessing her decision to go along while she peered at the passing homes. Many of the yards were festooned with elaborate Christmas displays. "We won't get into any trouble?"

"Nope. There's no way I'd have agreed to anything that could mess up your scholarship program."

"Okay."

Nick pointed to a specular grouping of red-hatted gnomes, their bodies made of evergreen boughs. "Wow, look at that those."

"And are *those* would be called a donsy of gnomes."

"Really, how do you know that?"

"I know lots of stuff. Now, don't miss our turn. It'll be the third house on the right."

"Me? Miss a turn?"

She leaned forward in her seat. "Do you see that?"

"See what?"

"Slow down. There's smoke coming from the chimney of our house."

"Think we smoked him out?"

"Terrible pun, Nick Parkos."

"No seriously, my gut's telling me something's happening." He passed the house, pulled over a couple doors down and grabbed his secure iPhone from the middle console. "I'm calling Geoff."

DEREK YANG THREW his final handful of shredded documents and the faux *Southern Living* magazine with the codes into the living room fireplace and dosed them with a squirt of lighter fluid. They burst into flame, sending a plume of dark-white smoke up the flue. The call from the Chinese Ministry of State Security operative had sent him into a panic. Amanda had been abducted. Probably by the American agents they'd had under surveillance.

He ran back to his study, tore open the back of his Mac,

lifted the black bar securing the hard drive, and yanked out the thin rectangular storage unit. He ran to the laundry room, emptied a bottle of bleach into the sink, and dropped in the drive. Absent his documents and information on his computer, he might have a chance...if he could get to his office in time.

ASTIN AVIATION
COLLEGE STATION, TEXAS
TUESDAY 21 DECEMBER

NICK PARKED in one of the designated stalls beside Astin Aviation's small terminal building. He grabbed their luggage and made for the nearest hangar as they'd been instructed. He and Michelle came to a halt before the open bay door. Before them was a sleek Gulfstream G550ER, its tail embossed with a gray and blue logo with a scripted "BTF." The colors of the logo matched those of a slash that ran along the fuselage. "Any idea what 'BTF' stands for?"

"'Better Than Fiction?'" Michelle ventured. She ran a professional eye over the aircraft. "You think this is Geoff's?"

He shook his head at another of his friend's mysteries that he hadn't uncovered with the background security checks he'd run after they'd first met at the Upper Crust Bar and Grill. "I have no idea, but it could explain how he gets around on such short notice. I've always harbored the suspicion he owns The Nicholas."

A uniformed man with four silver stripes on his dark-blue shoulder boards popped into view at the cabin door. He descended the stairs and extended his right hand. "I'm Jeff, your pilot. We'll pull chocks as soon as you're settled. Mr. Lange said to proceed without him and some of the others.

Loose ends to clean up. We'll come back and get them. Vinny and Jennifer should be here in a few."

"Navy?" Nick asked.

"F-18s."

They followed Jeff up the stairs where he introduced them to the flight attendant, Andy, before he disappeared into the cockpit.

Michelle surveyed the luxurious interior. "Geez, this tops Air Force One."

"You've been in the president's aircraft?" Andy asked.

"I used to be aircrew." She turned to Nick. "I met this guy on a return trip from Paris."

Nick ran his hand over a soft off-white leather seat while eyeing a plate of chocolates set on an adjoining table. "This is fancier than the jet Mike and I took to Denver on the last op."

Andy took a sniff of the cabin air. "Do I smell gingerbread?"

Michelle handed him a Christmas bag. "A thank you for you and the pilots."

He opened the bag. "Oh, boy. My favorites. I'm not sure the pilots will see any of these."

"It's a family recipe."

"On that note, let me give you the cook's tour. The chairs do all the usual stuff but can swivel, and they have a built-in massage function." He pressed a button on the remote he held. A burl-wood table top opened to reveal a flat screen TV. "We have three other zones, the next is the mini-bar, then the work area. The owner's suite is in the rear of the aircraft. If you're tired, I can make up the bed."

He grasped Michelle's hand. "How long is the flight?"

"About five hours, give or take," Michelle replied, "but don't be gettin' any ideas there, cowboy."

"Maybe we could fly around a bit, say to Hawaii?"

"Remember, the man said he has to come back and pick up the others," Michelle replied.

"Hey, y'all," Vinny said, announcing his and Jennifer's arrival with his southern drawl. "Nice, huh?"

"You could say that," Michelle said.

"Dibs on the owner's suite," Nick added.

Jennifer stepped around the guys and gave Michelle a hug. "It's yours. We've flown the BTF lots of times."

"BTF?" Michelle asked. "I saw it on the tail. What's it stand for?"

"Big Tough Frogman," Vinny clarified as he made for the second zone.

Nick joined him at the mini-bar. "Maybe we need to add the BTF to our Christmas wish list."

"We might make a play for it. Geoff owes us. We've got enough to nail Yang and take him off the streets."

∿

THE NICHOLAS
3138 M STREET NW
GEORGETOWN, WASHINGTON D.C.
WEDNESDAY 22, DECEMBER

"Excuse me, Jessica." Geoff Lange stood and scanned the second floor drawing room of The Nicholas from his usual place by the fireplace. He smiled at what he saw. Finally, the team could let its hair down and relax.

Nick and Michelle stood by the ten-foot blue spruce Christmas tree dominating the far corner of the room while chatting with their friends, Mike and Kate Rohrbaugh. Austin Mack was stationed behind a long serving table laden with his latest fabulous creations trading quips with Vinny. A burst of laughter came from the last grouping. Jennifer, Ann, and Marie. George was downstairs waiting on Vanatsky.

"Gunnar told me he might be running late," Jessica Caudry said from her chair positioned next to his in front of the hearth. "He texted. Said his debrief with the AAG went long."

Geoff nodded and took a moment to observe the others. The team had surprised him by transforming his man-cave. Fresh garlands woven with white mini-lights draped the mantel and the windows behind Austin. The fresh greenery permeated the room with the festive aroma of pine. He picked up a fire poker and gave the pile a stir. A festive mix of blue, yellow and green flames burst from the treated pinecones.

"*Nollarg Creidheil*! Merry Christmas, mates."

All eyes turned to Edmund, attired in full highland's regalia including hose flashing and the black leather sporran.

"You look dashing, Edmund," Michelle said.

"It's not often I get to wear my national garb." He stood aside. "And look what I found lurking a'boot the front door. Our way..." He flashed a smile at Jessica. "Well, our other wayward FBI special agent."

Gunnar Vanatsky exited the stairs, his eyes locking on the pile of presents stacked under the tree. "Sorry, I don't have a present for the exchange."

Edmund filled the brief silence that followed. "Aye, but you do have something as good. A solid win for the good guys."

"That's more than enough." George gestured to a side table festooned with an imposing collection of top-end brands of whisky, gin, and mixers. "Drink?"

"That'd be great. It's been a long day."

"What do ya have?" Vinny asked.

Vanatsky studied the scotch. "The Glennglassaugh Rival. I've never tried that one."

"Neat?"

"A couple drops of water."

Geoff caught the last of the exchange. "Good man. You know your scotch. There's hope yet for the FBI. You care for a cigar to go with your glass? We have a number of things to celebrate." He opened his humidor and offered one of his Pradron 50s without waiting for a response. "I understand the arrest warrant was unsealed."

"The U.S. District Court for the Southern District of Texas. Conspiring to act as an illegal agent for the Chinese."

Vinny hefted his glass. "Nailed the bastard."

"A solid win," Vanatsky affirmed, ticking off the charges on the fingers of his right hand. "Wire fraud, destruction of documents and evidence, tax evasion, failure to report income—"

"And AmpTex?" George asked.

"Deliberate and reckless disregard for the truth, but we're working a deal if they offer up all of Yang's data and can help us unearth the Chinese network."

"I'd say that's enough talk about work," Marie said. She grabbed Vanatsky's elbow, guiding him to Austin's magnificent buffet: Faux gras toasts, a selection of his family's artisanal cheese, a seafood tower, and at the end of the table, a pile of Michelle's ginger bread men.

"Lassies and lads," Edmund announced. "Before we indulge in Austin's repast, a celebratory poinsettia champagne cocktail is in order." With a flourish, he opened a cooler and extracted a bottle of chilled Cointreau and poured a wee dram into a champagne flute. "For the uninitiated, Cointreau has a milder flavor than Grand Marnier and is better suited for mixed drinks." He followed the orange liqueur with three ounces of cranberry juice and extracted another bottle from the cooler.

"And, a tip 'o the hat to the colonies." He popped open a

bottle of Chandon California Brut and handed it to Geoff. "As our host, will you do the honors?"

"Excellent sir," Edmund observed as Geoff topped off the flutes. To finish the cocktail, he dropped in a couple cranberries for the garnish, topped the lot with a small sprig of rosemary and handed the first to Michelle.

She took a sip. "Edmund this is fabulous. You ever think of going into another line of work?"

With a wink toward Geoff, he said. "Depends on my compensation."

With the clock nearing mid-night, Geoff pointed to Nick and Michelle and wrapped up the party. "We gotta get these young pups back home."

$\sim$

THE STATION APARTMENTS
COLLEGE STATION, TEXAS
SATURDAY 25 DECEMBER

NICK SAT cross-legged next to the small Christmas tree he'd purchased and that Michelle had helped him decorate the night before. She wore a pair of Victoria Secret white Christmas pajamas adorned with alternating horizontal bands of red snowflakes and ornaments, explaining that every Christmas eve her mom would gift her a new pair to be opened along with one present of her choosing.

"I can do that," he replied.

"I bet you can, tiger, but when we have kids, we'll stay with the modest long sleeves and legs."

He reached behind the tree, pulled out a small box, and held it just out of her reach.

"Ooh, you know I love surprises. Let me see. Let me see."

He handed over the box which she promptly put by her ear and shook. Her parents always accused her of being a savant, able to guess what was in all of her wrapped packages.

"Is it an ornament?"

"Maybe."

"What kind?"

"Not telling."

She slipped off the bow and the wrapping paper, tossing both aside. Staring back at her through a clear plastic window were a pair of large, round, yellow eyes. "Oh, it's Hedwig." She wrapped her arms around him, then drew back and hung Hedwig on the tree. "He doesn't quite go with the other ornaments, but he'll always have a place of honor."

"We might have to start another Christmas tradition."

"You betcha. Now how about some of Edmund's Athol Bross?"

"Gah, that's a tradition I may have to take a pass on. How 'bout some eggnog?"

"Ah, come on. It'd grow on you."

"Will it grow hair on my chest?"

"Not likely." She reached for his hand. "You want a blob?" she asked, using her term for the irregular round cookies she'd made from the leftover scraps of rolled gingerbread dough.

"I get the one with all the icing."

She jumped up with a laugh and ran to the kitchen. "Not if I get it first."

CHAPTER 5
YULETIDE SPLITSVILLE
BY WILLIAM BERNHARDT

(This story takes place between *Exposed* and *Shameless* in the Splitsville legal thriller series)

K enzi held the refrigerator door open to block her guests' view of what she was doing on the other side. They were busy. They wouldn't notice. She hoped. Her daughter, Hailee, was showing her sister, Emma, and her assistant, Sharon, a beautiful red and green scarf. Hailee had crocheted it herself—and many others just like it. Did Emma and Sharon realize there was an identical scarf under the tree for each of them? If not, they would soon.

Kenzi opened the bottle and quietly poured the contents into a pitcher. She didn't know why she was being so secretive. Must be related to some deep-seated insecurity. They all knew she couldn't cook. But Sharon had challenged her to make the eggnog from scratch, and she could never resist a challenge. She read an online article that suggested it was easy—and then proceeded to give lengthy, complicated instructions about whisking and heating that were completely over her head. Which one of these metal thingies was the whisk? Hailee would know, but she wasn't going to blow her cover by asking. This ready-to-drink bottle she snagged at Capco even included the liquor. She didn't have to do anything. But she stirred a little, for show. She even set out an empty egg carton and some cream.

She put three glasses on a tray and carried them to the living room of her spacious downtown Seattle apartment. "Okay, time to get merry. Eggnog, Kenzi-style."

Her friends grabbed their glasses. "I feel merrier already," Sharon said, laughing. Her dark face brightened and she brought the glass to her lips.

"I normally abstain from alcoholic beverages," Emma said. She was, as usual, decked out in black Goth attire, though she was sporting a tiny reindeer brooch. "But whatever. It's Christmas."

Kenzi was impressed. Just getting the normally reclusive Emma to a social gathering was no small feat. If Emma actually appeared to enjoy herself, well, the Christmas spirit really was contagious.

Emma licked her lips. "What's the liquor in it?"

"What's the—?" Kenzi froze. It would be too obvious if she went back into the kitchen to read the label. "It's...rum."

"Huh. Tastes like some kind of brandy."

"Well...it's a...brandy rum."

Sharon frowned. "That's not a thing. You're mixing grape and grain."

Kenzi raised her chin. "I'm not revealing my secret recipe. Does it taste good?"

"It does, actually."

"Then what else matters?"

"Hey, where's mine?" Hailee peered up from her wheel-chair, obviously unhappy. Though she could walk in short spurts, she suffered from ME—myalgic encephalomyelitis—which meant she tired easily and had to be careful not to exhaust herself.

Kenzi shook her head. "You're only fourteen, dear. I'll have some eggnog ready for you in seven years."

"Didn't you put some aside before you added the booze?" Hailee sat beside their small Christmas tree, which she had decorated with biodegradable, eco-friendly, no Red Dye #3, recyclable, non-plastic ornaments. Probably gluten-free, for all Kenzi knew. "Like that crappy sparkling grape juice you feed me on New Year's?"

"Sorry. Didn't think of that." Because it would be impossible. Because the bottle came with the booze already added. "I can get you some orange juice."

"Right. Because that's practically the same thing."

Kenzi ignored her. "Thanks for coming over, everyone. I know you have other things to do on Christmas Eve. But I thought it would be nice if we all spent an hour or two together before we went our separate ways." She raised a glass. "I want to propose a toast to—"

"We can't have a toast," Hailee said, cutting her off.

"We can if you don't interrupt your mother again."

"We can't have a toast because I don't have a glass."

"Hailee—"

"Here," Emma said, "take mine." She glanced at Kenzi. "Just for show purposes." Then glanced back at Hailee and winked.

Kenzi frowned. "I feel I'm losing control of this situation."

Sharon laughed. "Girl, you were never in control of this situation."

"And I've forgotten my toast."

"Allow me." Sharon raised her glass. "Here's to Team Kenzi, the roughest toughest legal team in Seattle. Mistresses of Mayhem. Demons of Divorce Court."

"With the occasional murder trial tossed in for spice," Emma added.

"Right. Spice. It's like...like the nutmeg on this eggnog." Sharon paused. "There is nutmeg in this eggnog. Right, Kenzi?"

"Umm...sure." Probably? She had no idea.

"Did the recipe call for nutmeg? Did you go to the store and purchase nutmeg?"

"What is this, an inquisition? Just drink it already!"

"You seem a little...edgy."

"I'm not edgy. I'm never edgy."

"Uh huh." Sharon gave her a long look, then moved on. "Have you livestreamed your holiday greetings to the KenziKlan?"

"Of course she has," Hailee said. "I'd be a poor social media manager if I allowed her to slack off on a day when most people are sitting at home with nothing to do. She sent out a warm ecumenical interfaith greeting that encompassed all and offended none."

"Kenzi didn't offend anyone? That doesn't sound like the girl I've been working with all these years."

"She's improving," Hailee set down the glass which, judging from her milk mustache, she had definitely sampled. "Under my tutelage. Are you visiting family for Christmas, Sharon?"

"No. We've fallen out of the habit. Since my siblings and I became adults. And by the way, you're being culturally insensitive. I celebrate Kwanzaa."

Hailee look stricken. "Oh. Gosh. I'm so sorry. I—"

Sharon waved a hand in the air. "I'm just messin' with you. My granddaddy was a Southern Baptist preacher. Of course I celebrate Christmas. Kwanzaa doesn't even start until January 26. I have Kwanzaa while you folks have Boxing Day, which is a lot better than a weird holiday no one understands."

"But not with your family?"

"We do our own thing during the holidays. I was thinking about flying down to St. Peterburg. See some friends, soak in some warm weather. You guys going to see Daddy Dearest?" Sharon was referring to Kenzi and Emma's father, Alejandro Rivera, the senior partner at the law firm where they both worked, known around town as "Splitsville" because they primarily handled divorce cases. Sharon knew all too well that Kenzi and her father had a rocky relationship. They were both strong-willed, determined control freaks, each eternally frustrated by their inability to control the other.

"Are you kidding?" Kenzi said. "I have to deal with that man every workday. I'm drawing the line at Christmas. Is Gabe going?" Gabriel was her younger brother, currently managing partner at the firm.

"I don't think so. He's hosting some bar association party. Always networking." Emma pursed her lips. "I wouldn't actually mind attending midnight mass."

"That's because Daddy doesn't constantly hassle you about your billables."

"Because he doesn't care what I do. And I'm not back-sliding into criminal law."

"It's not backsliding. It's expanding my portfolio. And helping women who seriously need—" She glanced toward the kitchen. "Something is burning."

Sharon's forehead wrinkled. "Are you pretending to cook again?"

Emma smiled. "Is defrosting considered cooking?"

"I heard that!" Kenzi raced into the kitchen, clattered

around for a few moments, then returned with a steaming tray. "Guess what we're having for Christmas lunch?"

Emma tilted her head to one side. "Probably goose."

Sharon shook her head. "Turkey."

"Turkey is Thanksgiving. Christmas is goose."

"Goose? No one has goose anymore."

"It's traditional at Christmastime."

"Where? In a Dickens novel?"

"In all your better homes."

"You're telling me your parents served goose at Christmastime?"

"No. Red pork tamales. Chicken pozole verde."

Hailee pulled a face. "Ick. Meat."

Emma smiled. "I'm sure your mother made some tofu mess just for you."

"Sure. Like she had something for me to drink."

"That was just an—" Emma eyebrows knitted. "Hey! My glass is empty."

Hailee looked away. "Losing track of your drinking is a red flag. Maybe you should see someone."

"Maybe I should keep a closer eye on my niece."

Kenzi interrupted. "Come to the table already. Partake of my splendid vegetarian Christmas meatloaf."

Sharon gave her a long look. "Are you kidding me?"

"What?"

"Honey, no one actually likes meatloaf. Even the kind that has meat in it."

"It doesn't need meat. It has nuts, rice, mushrooms, onions, herbs, cheese..."

"At least you memorized the list of ingredients before you took it out of the box."

She wanted to protest, but she knew they'd never believe

her. "Ok, I got it from Whole Foods. All I had to do was heat it up. But that doesn't mean it isn't good."

"To the contrary. I'm relieved that it came from Whole Foods."

"I feel you lack faith in my cooking skills."

"That's because you don't have any cooking skills."

"I could've made this. If I'd had time..."

"You couldn't make this any more than you could make the eggnog. And I—" Sharon glanced down. A puzzled expression crossed her face. "Pardon me. It's my mother." She pulled her phone to her ear and muttered in low tones.

Now that Kenzi thought about it, she didn't recall Sharon ever mentioning her mother, which was amazing given how long they'd worked together. She tried not to eavesdrop, but the temptation was overwhelming. Something about the sound of whispering always attracted more attention.

Sharon's voice rose. "On Christmas Eve?" Pause. "Okay. I'll be right over." Sharon disconnected and put the phone back in her pocket. "I'm sorry, Kenzi. Keep a piece of meatloaf warm for me. I need to go to my parents' place."

"Is...everything okay?"

"Not remotely." She ran her fingers through her hair. "My mother's prize possession has disappeared. A pearl necklace. Wedding gift from my father. By far the most valuable thing she has. I think it's worth more than their house. And now it's gone."

"That's terrible. Your mother must be very upset."

"You could say that." Sharon looked up abruptly. "She says without that necklace, she doesn't have a marriage."

"But—that can't—"

"She says if it doesn't turn up, she's filing for divorce."

Kenzi's jaw lowered. She could barely follow this, much less make sense of it. "But—that—"

"Yeah. I know. And a merry Christmas to you too."

KENZI TRIED to learn as much as possible about this domestic crisis during the drive to Sharon's parents' place. She'd been reluctant to join this expedition, but Sharon begged her to come and see if she could figure out what happened to the necklace. She still didn't feel right about leaving her daughter and sister on Christmas Eve, but Hailee insisted she needed to help her friend, and Emma agreed to stay with Hailee till she returned.

"My dad was stationed overseas," Sharon explained as she drove. "After he came back stateside, he had trouble finding work. Spent a year as the janitor at a high school, then got on as a sanitation worker. Did that for years till he finally swung a desk job with the highway department. My mom was cleaning houses, but with Dad's newfound stability, she decided to go to school. Got an associates' degree and qualified as a substance abuse treatment specialist. Her patients love her. I've heard people gush about how she saved their lives."

"That's wonderful." Kenzi scanned the neighborhood. This was Duvall, a modest-but-nice Seattle suburb. While this particular street wasn't ritzy, it certainly wasn't poor. "I don't mean to be rude, but nothing about your parents' backstory suggests the means to buy an expensive pearl necklace."

"He won it in a poker game, while he was still in the army. He and Mom say the necklace made their marriage possible. Even though they didn't sell it. Gave him credibility or something. They knew they'd never starve as long as they had the necklace. It's like a symbol for the whole relationship."

"So if the necklace disappears..."

"Exactly." She made a hard right. "We have to find it, Kenzi. We have to."

"This is not exactly my usual line of work."

"Don't sell yourself short. You've become quite adept at solving puzzles."

Kenzi sighed. Yes, she'd been lucky once or twice, but she definitely wasn't ready for her deerstalker cap. Emma was better read. Hailee was much smarter. She felt like she was here under false pretenses. "What else do you know about the necklace?"

"I'm no gemologist," Sharon said, "but I've heard them talk about it often enough. It's a beautiful single pink pearl, teardrop-shape, hanging like a pendant and surrounded with little diamonds. If I remember correctly, it's an abalone pearl, over 200 carats."

Kenzi whistled. Okay, maybe she was qualified for this case. Because she loved to accessorize. And she knew any pearl that size would have a five-digit price tag. At least.

Sharon continued. "It has natural pastel pink hues, but you can also see iridescent flashes of blue, green, silver. Maybe a little orange. Dad thought it originated in Australia, but apparently it passed through many hands before it came to him." She pulled up in front of an attractive one-story house with carefully trimmed hedges. Kenzi guessed maybe 2000 square feet. "We've arrived."

Kenzi followed Sharon to the front door, but before they arrived, a woman emerged who looked for all the world like an older, thicker version of Sharon. She had a bounce in her step and a smile on her face which, given the circumstances, Kenzi found impressive.

Sharon hugged her mother and introduced Kenzi. Kenzi offered a hand, but the woman brushed it aside and swallowed her up in a huge bearhug. "Call me Bertha," she said. "I'm so glad you could join us."

"I'm sorry you're...experiencing some unhappiness."

Bertha's eyebrows pushed together. "This has been...very hard. But I'm glad you're here. It's been a long while since we saw the kids on Christmas. And Sharon never brought a guest before."

"I'm glad to finally meet you. Sharon and I have been friends for years."

Bertha nodded. "And when you say you're friends..." Her eyebrows danced.

It took Kenzi a moment to follow. "Oh—do you mean—are we—oh no. We're—I mean, I'm—"

"Just friends, Mom," Sharon said, giving her a look that was indescribable. "We work together."

"Oh, fine, fine." Bertha fluttered her hands in the air. "But you know, it's all okay with me. I just want my children to be happy."

Sharon's eyes darted skyward. "I know, Mom. And I want you to be happy. So let's find the necklace before you become one of Kenzi's clients."

They stepped inside. Like the exterior, the family room was not ornate or cluttered with expensive tchotchkes, but it was clean and well kept. Spare but tasteful. She spotted a breakfront near the door displaying some fine china—and an empty space with a barren jewelry stand. Is that where the necklace used to be? They had two Christmas trees, both about four feet tall. His-and-her trees? One appeared to be decorated with spaceships. Closer inspection confirmed that it was a Star Trek-themed tree. His, she surmised. The other tree, with more traditional ornaments, must be Bertha's.

"Admiring my tree?" She looked up and saw a tall man

with gray-flecked hair standing beside her. "I'm Chad. Sharon's dad. You must be Kenzi."

"I am." She glanced at the tree. "Star Trek fan?"

"I've been collecting those Hallmark ornaments for years. Some of them are quite valuable now. The Borg cube is the prize of my collection."

She assumed he was referring to the gray square ornament. "It does stand out. And your wife keeps her own tree?"

He chuckled, a deep-throated laugh. "You know what they say. Women like jewelry. Boys like spaceships."

Did anyone actually say that? "Sharon told me you celebrate Christmas *and* Kwanzaa."

"Why not have the best of both worlds? I wouldn't cheat my kids out of Santa and presents. But why not also remember our African heritage? I have friends who feel Christmas is a white holiday and we should just celebrate our own past, but I respectfully disagree. We live in this world. We should be a part of it, at least as much as possible."

"Sharon told me Kwanzaa starts after Christmas. And goes on for..."

"Seven days. Each day is dedicated to a different principle: unity, self-determination, responsibility, community, purpose, creativity, and faith."

Kenzi pointed at an end table bearing a candle holder with seven candles. "Is this part of the festivities?"

Chad smiled. "That's the Kinara. Fancy word for a candle holder. One candle for each day."

"Sounds like a lovely tradition."

"We think so. People call it a made-up holiday, but I think it's just as real as people want it to be. You know, Clinton made Kwanzaa an officially recognized holiday. We even have Kwanzaa Hallmark cards now!"

Bertha called from across the room. "Chad! Stop boring our

guest with your long lectures. Introduce her to the rest of the family."

"Yes, ma'am."

Chad escorted her toward the small sitting area, just two facing sofas and a recliner. The recliner was empty, but that was probably Chad's special chair, so she walked past it. Bertha darted into the kitchen and Sharon followed, which left her alone with the rest of the family.

A slender man in a Santa sweatshirt rose. "I'm Lionel. Sharon's little brother." He jabbed a thumb to the right. "And this is my fiancée, Amanda."

Amanda was white, pale white even, with blonde hair. Kenzi was not one to engage in fat-shaming and believed all women should have positive body images. But Amanda was carrying about forty pounds more than she needed, and she didn't know how anyone could be happy about that.

"Pleased to meet you," Amanda said, though Kenzi didn't sense she meant it. Her expression was more like, Why the hell are you here?

The woman beside Amanda rose. "I'm the eldest child. Sharon's big sis. Jean." She was shorter than everyone else in the family, and yet, Kenzi got the impression that didn't slow her down much. "Just for the record, I was against inviting outsiders. This is a family matter. It should be handled by family."

"I don't mean to intrude."

"I hardly think you're here by accident."

"I'm just saying—"

"We have no need for professionals."

"I'm not here as a lawyer—"

"But you are a lawyer. Right? In that firm Sharon slaves for? I wouldn't be surprised if you went home and billed us for your time."

Kenzi's teeth clenched. Tolerance was a virtue, but she drew the line at lawyer hate speech. Nonetheless, she tried to remain civil. "I'm just here to support Sharon. She wanted—"

"I pushed Sharon to get a four-year degree, but she didn't see the need." Jean let out a bitter chuckle. "Apparently she's content to be a secretary her entire life."

"Sharon is not a secretary. She's my assistant, and she handles all kinds of top-level professional matters. She's an equal member of my team."

Jean arched an eyebrow. "You mean the KenziKlan?"

She was surprised and somewhat taken aback. "No, that's an online group. Did Sharon mention it to you?"

"I try to stay on top of what's happening in my family. I even listened to your livestream once. For a few minutes, anyway. You dispense a lot of advice."

Kenzi didn't take the bait. "My work constantly reminds me that many women are hurting. We all need to help one another."

"And that's why you're butting into my family's business?"

"I...yes. Actually."

"Don't get in the way. I'm supervising this investigation, which has already begun without your assistance."

"Understood," she replied, without explaining that what she understood was that this psycho-typical eldest daughter liked to be in charge and had a pronounced case of sibling rivalry.

She edged away from Jean, which put her practically in the lap of an older man sitting on the opposite sofa. He was also African-American, and thin, almost skeletal.

He didn't rise, but he did extend a hand. "My name is Bass. Robert Bass. Next door neighbor." He grinned. "One of those outsiders Jean was talking about."

Kenzi shook his hand. "Kenzi Rivera."

"Rivera. So you're Mexican."

Kenzi stiffened. "My family is Latinx."

"I don't even know what that means. Why do people think they have to make up words? What's wrong with the old words?"

"It's a gender-neutral term indicating that my ancestors came from somewhere else. Just like your ancestors. What brings you here?"

"Chad asked me to come over. I was glad to get out of the house. I lost my job at the factory not too long ago. Now I sit around and watch Fox News all day. Hey—do you know Geraldo Rivera? I think he's like you. Latinish."

"Latinx."

"What you said."

Chad cut in. "Kenzi, you still haven't met one member of the family."

Kenzi whirled around. He was holding a big black cat with white paws.

"This is Gus."

Kenzi smiled. "Is he a theater cat?"

"I see you know your poetry. Or your musicals."

"Or both." Kenzi petted the big black bundle of fur. "What a darling. I bet he gets into all kinds of mischief."

"Oh, he sleeps mostly, rising occasionally to eat and bat his stuffed mouse across the floor. Would you care to have a drink with me in my office? I just whipped up a batch of eggnog."

She blinked. "You made it yourself?"

"Sure. It isn't hard."

Okay, now she hated him. "Lead the way."

∽

KENZI FOLLOWED Chad down the hallway and into a small room. It looked like it had been a bedroom, but once this house became an empty nest, he converted it into a small office. Or mancave. A place he could call his own.

He plopped down behind the desk and gestured for Kenzi to take the other available chair. "My own secret recipe," Chad said, as he dipped the ladle into a punchbowl and poured it into a mug. "Wanna know the secret ingredient?"

"Okay."

He peered deep into her eyes. "Nutmeg."

She blinked. "Isn't that...somewhat standard?"

"I don't mean putting it in. I mean leaving it out. What difference does it make? If you've put in enough rum, no one's gonna notice." He scooted the mug across the table to her.

"So you use rum. Not brandy."

"I see you're an eggnog connoisseur."

"Not really." She raised the mug gingerly and took a tiny sip. This wasn't a good time to fuzz up her head, and she was beginning to hate eggnog. "Mmm. Very good."

"Tis the season to be jolly. Have some more."

"I will." Later.

"I looooove this time of year. I love Christmas. And Kwanzaa. And Hanukkah, for that matter, even though I don't know the first thing about it. Anything that causes people to focus on being nice for a change. But let's face it—Christmas has the best tunes." He began to sing—if you could call it that. "Deck the halls with boughs of holly, fa-la-la-la-la-la-la-la-la-la..."

His aria had a few too many la's in it. Which made her wonder if he'd started sampling the eggnog before company came. "Can you tell me more about the necklace? Sharon says it's sort of a...central artifact for your marriage."

"That's a nice way of putting it. I've never had it appraised, but I know it's worth some serious simoleons. Bertha was hesitant about hitching her star to me until I gave her that baby. I mean, I got her a ring, too. But it paled by comparison. That's when Bertha took the plunge. I think she reasoned that even if I proved to be the worthless no-account her father said I was, we could always pawn the necklace."

"You got it overseas?"

He nodded. "Okinawa. Did my part for the red, white, and blue. Picked up a few skills too, not that they helped me find work when I came back stateside. At first, I had nothing but a uniform and two changes of underwear. And a foot locker."

As if on cue, Bertha entered. "Where he keeps his porn."

Chad slapped a hand on the desk. "That is not true!"

Bertha waved a hand in the air. "Don't bother. I've gone through that thing. Old love letters. The uniform you keep even though you couldn't possibly fit into it. And your porn."

Chad was visibly irritated. "Are you referring to my collection of classic Tijuana Bibles?"

"Porn."

"Classic comics." He glanced across the desk at Kenzi, as if pleading for an intervention. "Do you know what Tijuana Bibles are?"

"I feel I should. But I don't."

"Little comic books. Same size as those religious tracts you see around sometimes. Very popular during the Depression. Often made unauthorized use of comic characters or movie stars. Mae West. Clark Gable. Famous people."

Bertha was unmoved. "Famous people having sex."

"They're more satirical than anything else. "

"Porn. Mae West should've sued."

"Why? It was an honor to know you were the subject of people's fantasies."

"Yeah, I know that's always been my dream. Illiterate bozos getting off on a cartoon version of myself."

"Tijuana Bibles are worth a lot of money."

"Good. Sell them."

Chad pointed a finger. "And you should not have been in my foot locker. A man deserves to have some privacy in his own home."

"So he can stash his porn."

Chad looked as if he were about to explode. "Collectibles. Like my Star Trek ornaments. And I thought we had an agreement. I stay out of your clothes closet and you stay out of my foot locker."

"There's an exception for porn." Bertha wrapped her arms around him. "Calm down, Chad. Can't you tell when you're being teased?" She looked at Kenzi and shrugged. "Men. Can't live with 'em, can't sell 'em for parts. I'm going back to—" She stopped short, then stumbled.

Kenzi sprang up. "What? What's wrong?"

Bertha was staring at the floor. "*Gus!* What are you doing?"

The black cat skittered away.

"He's out to get me," Bertha muttered. "I can see it in his yellow eyes."

"They do say black cats are bad luck," Kenzi noted.

"Especially when they want to kill you. Do you have pets, Kenzi?"

"No. Not an option. We live in an apartment near my office."

"Wise." Bertha poured herself some eggnog. Kenzi noticed her hand trembled. "No lawn to mow. No pipes to repair. And no cats."

"Are you okay?"

Bertha took a sip, her hand still shaking. "This whole necklace business has me upset. I didn't sleep at all last night. Kept flipping from one position to another."

"I told you what I think," Chad said. His face had not

relaxed since the Tijuana Bible discussion. "It was that blonde woman. Amanda."

"Stop. We all know you don't want your precious only son to marry her. It doesn't make her a thief."

"Golddigger. Sure as the world."

"Based on what? Her skin color?"

"You know I don't care about that. But she doesn't have a job. How does she pay her rent? I think she wants a sugar daddy."

"And our boy needs a wife. Something to stabilize him. He could still make his mark in this world, if he'd stop messing around."

"I don't trust her. She's got a chip on her shoulder."

"Are you talking about Amanda or our eldest?"

"Don't you go dissing our Jean. That girl has been the apple of my eye since the day she was born and you know it."

"That apple is only in your eye because you're wearing rose-colored glasses."

"Bertha—"

Kenzi thought this might be a good time to create a diversion. "May I ask who had access to the necklace?"

Bertha shrugged. "Probably everyone in the family. They all have keys. They could've come while we were away. It would be easy to do."

Chad pushed himself out of his chair. "Are you calling our children thieves?"

"I'm just saying it's possible."

"Don't go accusing people without cause."

"Like you just did to Amanda?"

"That's different. She's not family."

"Not yet."

Kenzi tried to get them back on track. "When did you notice the necklace was missing?"

"Yesterday," Bertha replied. "I should've called everyone then, but I wanted to make sure there wasn't a logical explanation. Like Chad took it out to be cleaned or something. But today I realized it wasn't going to miraculously reappear. And this couldn't come at a worse time."

Kenzi cocked her head. "Meaning..."

Bertha and Chad exchanged a look. "We might as well tell her the truth," Bertha said. "Chad got laid off. Early retirement, they say, but the benefits aren't great. And my business isn't doing what it once was. We're going to have a hard time making ends meet."

Kenzi tried to drink it all in. "And that's when the necklace disappeared..."

Bertha looked at her sharply. "Are you thinking I swiped it? Sold it? Well, I didn't. I would never. Some things are more important than money. But it's gone, just the same. So I called all the kids." She paused. "And started packing my bag."

"You're...leaving?"

Bertha held up her hand. "Don't start. I know it doesn't make sense to other people. But it does to me. Without that necklace, there's no marriage. And no reason to stay."

Sharon entered. "Hey! Can't you smell that? Something in the kitchen is burning."

"Damn. Seems like I can't smell anything anymore." She raced to the kitchen. Kenzi followed close behind, with the other two trailing.

Bertha went straight to the oven. A wave of steam blew out. She retrieved a large roasting pan. "No one's going to complain that the turkey is underdone. But I think it may still be edible. You can rejoin your siblings, Sharon. I bet you're having fun catching up."

"Is that what you call it? More like refereeing."

"Don't tell me you kids are squabbling again."

"I don't squabble. I'm a grown adult." Sharon glanced sideways at Kenzi. "But that doesn't mean bossy big sis can't get on my nerves."

Bertha made a tsking noise. "No matter how old they get, some things never change."

"Because Jean never changes. She's got a mean streak."

"And you've got a rebellious streak."

"Mom, it is not my fault—"

Bertha raised her hands, which somehow had the effect of cutting Sharon off mid-sentence. "It's Christmas Eve. I want my family to love each other. I don't need any more stress. I've got enough already and my doctor says this stress is the worst thing for me right now. So please let's have a pleasant evening where we remember that we're one family and we share the same DNA and that means we should all love one another."

Kenzi could see Sharon's teeth gnashing, but she kept her lips buttoned. "Sharon, why don't you help your mom get dinner on? I'm useless in the kitchen. I'd like to chat with your siblings."

"Better you than me," Sharon replied.

Bertha cupped her hand to her ear. "What did you say, Sharon?"

"Nothing," Sharon muttered. "Nothing at all."

KENZI INTENDED to settle on the sofa, but as soon as she left the kitchen she heard someone outside shouting.

Jean looked up. "No worries. It's just Lionel and his alleged fiancée. They do this a lot."

"Family visits can be stressful."

"Their relationship is stressful. But they keep clinging to it by their fingernails. I mean, I get why Amanda's in it. She needs a financier. But Lionel could be with anyone. If he showed a little more backbone."

Yes, Kenzi thought, you are definitely the oldest child. And then froze in mid-thought. Because in her family, she was the oldest child. "I'm going outside."

Jean waved a hand in the air. "Don't say I didn't warn you."

Lionel and Amanda had moved to the side of the house, slightly less visible, but hardly out of sight. "Everything okay?"

Lionel and Amanda looked up abruptly.

"We're fine," Lionel said. "Just mapping out our holiday plans."

"There's more?"

Lionel shrugged. "My fiancée thinks we should visit her parents. I think we should stay here. At least till after dinner."

Kenzi hesitated. She didn't want to get in the middle of it. But... "I hope you can stay a little longer. Your mother is very upset. She's talking about leaving your father."

Amanda chuckled slightly. "After all these years? Where would she go?"

"I don't know. Apparently they're having money problems too."

Lionel and Amanda glanced at one another. Amanda was the first to break the silence. "That takes care of Plan A."

"You had a plan?"

Lionel's eyes darted downward. "We were going to...you know...ask my parents for a small loan. Just to get our married life off to the right start. There are some things Amanda thinks we need."

"You should see his kitchen," Amanda said, as if she thought Kenzi, being female, would be a sympathetic ear. If she'd realized how limited Kenzi's cooking skills were, she wouldn't have bothered. "He barely has plates. No crockpot. No mixer. No runner on the kitchen table. His bowls look like something you'd use to feed the cat." Her voice rose. "He doesn't even have a coffeemaker!"

"I can see where that would be a problem."

"It's all a problem. We're going to need new furniture. Gardening. A new bed. I'm not sleeping on the mattress you shared with all those floozies."

Lionel's eyes widened. "I had floozies?"

"If you want me to be your wife, you need to learn how to treat me right."

Kenzi tried to sound sympathetic. "Sounds like you two could use a financial infusion yourselves."

Amanda folded her arms across her chest. "That's the only reason we're here."

Lionel muttered. "Only reason you're here."

"Lionel," Kenzi said, "when was the last time you visited your parents?"

"I don't know. A couple of months ago. Why?"

"You do have a key, right?"

"What are you suggesting?"

"Only the obvious. You had access."

"Meaning?"

Amanda offered an unnecessary explanation. "She's saying you're a suspect, you numbskull. You could've taken the necklace."

"You think I'd steal from my own mother?"

Kenzi shook her head. "I'm exploring possibilities."

"Who the hell do you think—"

"For that matter, Amanda, you've been sleeping over at Lionel's place, right?"

Amanda appeared outraged. "What is this? Slut-shaming?"

"Far from it. I'm just noting that you had access to Lionel's keys. You could've gotten up in the night and made a copy. Come over when his parents were away."

"Where do you get off accusing—"

"I haven't accused anyone of anything. That's not my style." She peered deeply into Amanda's eyes. "I collect facts. And then when I'm ready, I reveal the truth."

When Kenzi reentered the house, Jean was rearranging the plates in the breakfront.

"I've told my mother a thousand times how these should be displayed. But she always messes it up."

Kenzi was perplexed. "Does it matter?"

"Of course it does. The most valuable ones should be on top."

"How do you know which ones are the most valuable?"

"You have to know something about blue-flow Spode. Which I guess you don't."

"I'm somewhat surprised your mother has fancy china."

"Only because I've given it to her. A new plate every year on her birthday."

"Does she like them?"

"I don't know. Her tastes tend to be more...plebian. I'm trying to give her something that will increase in value. In case the time comes when...she needs it."

"Like if she leaves your father?"

Jean closed the breakfront doors. "Why do you say that?"

"Are you aware that your mother has packed her bag?"

"No..."

"And apparently your parents are in a financial crunch."

"I did know that." Jean shook her head. "The necklace could've helped."

"If they'd been willing to sell it. Your mother seems to think her whole marriage rides on that one pink teardrop."

"Probably because it's the only thing she's ever had that was worth anything. Other than these plates. Which she doesn't appreciate." Jean sighed. "Father has never treated her like she deserves. He'd be nothing without her. He'd probably still be in the army. Or dead."

"I'm sure he does the best he can."

"No. He doesn't. Doesn't even try. Too lazy. Too determined to be the nice guy. It's a sham."

It was hard to hear a daughter speak so poorly of her father. Especially so soon after she'd heard the father speak so glowingly about his daughter. "Taking care of a family is hard."

"Hard for him. Not for others. I've told Mother she should leave him. Move in with me. Let me take care of things. She's too old for this crap. Did you know she manages the household expenses?"

"I did not."

"She has to. Father is worthless when it comes to money. I'm not even sure he has basic math skills. I just hope she isn't dipping into her legacy."

"Legacy?"

"Some money my grandmother left Mother a year or so ago. It's not a fortune, but it's enough for a lifestyle upgrade. I bet she hasn't even invested it wisely."

"Have you asked her?"

"Not directly. I don't think she understands anything about money. She just needs to turn it all over to me."

"You want to be in charge of her legacy?"

"Is there something wrong with that? What's the point of having children if, eventually, they can't take charge of the day-to-day crap so you don't have to?"

Sounded good. But when Kenzi looked into Jean's eyes, she got a feeling her motives were less altruistic. "What is it you do again?"

"I'm an HR manager at DigiDynamics. It's a tech firm—"

"I'm familiar with it. They had a lot of layoffs recently, didn't they? When Morgan Moreno took charge?"

"What's your point?"

"No point. Just asking questions."

Jean did not attempt to mask her hostility. "Shouldn't you be off at mass somewhere?"

"Excuse me?"

"You're Catholic, right?"

"Technically..."

"You Hispanics are so predictable."

Kenzi's neck tensed. "I'm not actually that religious. But I think it's good for my daughter to—"

"You've made a bundle off other people's personal problems, haven't you?"

"I've—*what?*"

"You're a divorce lawyer, aren't you?"

"Usually. But what you said before was wrong. I don't even bill by the hour. I—"

"I'm sure you have some scheme for getting rich. How else could you afford that outfit you're wearing? You rake in the big bucks and pay my sister as little as possible."

"Actually, Sharon just got a big—" She paused. "Is there some reason you're putting me on trial?"

Jean smiled. "Is there some reason that, just a moment ago, you were putting me on trial?"

Robert couldn't have picked a more opportune moment to step in. "Hey, what're you two gals yakking about?"

"Nothing important," Kenzi said. "I'm glad you could be here today, Robert. I can see the family trusts you."

Jean rolled her eyes.

"Do you know anything about this necklace business?"

"No more than anyone else. I used to be a PI, once upon a

time, so Chad asked me to take a look into things. But I didn't get very far."

"That's a big favor to ask."

"You ain't a-jokin'. I mean, housesitting, sure. Happy to do it. But this is something else again. I can't figure why anyone would want to take that necklace."

Jean snorted. "Money."

"Well now, not everything can be reduced to dollars and cents, young lady. What that pearl meant to Chad and Bertha—that can't be bought at the store. That can't be borrowed from the bank. I saw what a difference it made to their lives."

"You knew Chad and Bertha before they were married?"

"Heck, yeah. Chad and I served together. In the army. I worshipped that man." He smiled. "Still think mighty highly of him."

They were interrupted by a loud cry from the kitchen. Sounded like Sharon and her mother both speaking at the same time. "Dinner!"

Kenzi pressed her hands together. "Thank goodness. Let's eat."

KENZI EXCUSED herself while the others prepared the dinner table. Chad slipped in two leaves to extend the length of the table so all eight guests could sit together. Sharon and Jean set the table, complete with Christmas crackers and lit candles in the Kinara. Kenzi returned and they all took their seats. They sat elbow-to-elbow and the end chairs touched walls on both sides, but since Chad and Bertha occupied those seats, she didn't have to worry about it.

Kenzi sat on one side between Sharon and Jean (she

thought it best to separate them) while Lionel, Amanda, and Robert faced them.

Bertha placed the turkey in the center of the table. It smelled delicious. If it had burned, she couldn't tell. She wondered if she should hazard a bite. Hailee had been pressuring her to "end her lifelong commitment to animal cruelty and save the planet in the process" by giving up meat. But Hailee wasn't here, and she thought she could trust Sharon to keep her mouth shut.

"What a feast!" Sharon said. "Mom, you're going to have a hard time topping this on Karamu." She leaned toward Kenzi. "That's the big Kwanzaa communal feast. On the sixth day. What the rest of the world calls New Year's Eve."

"You give up New Year's Eve?"

"It's an important part of our culture. Can't miss the feast."

Bertha smiled. "And Sharon usually slips out before midnight for a drink or two."

"Mom!"

"Or so I've heard." She looked down at her food. "I wouldn't know. I don't remember the last time we were all gathered like this at the holidays. One last time."

Chad stabbed a fork in his turkey. "Bertha, would you stop acting as if the world is coming to an end? It's just a necklace."

"It is so so so much more than just a necklace."

Kenzi cut in. "I'm sure it will turn up. Give it time. Don't do anything drastic."

"Time isn't infinite."

"No, but this dressing sure is." Robert helped himself to a huge spoonful. "You do a fine job with the fixins."

"Thank you, Robert."

"Chad, you remember that Thanksgiving we spent in Okinawa?"

"I do. Worst holiday ever."

"But best dressing ever. Till tonight."

Amanda chimed in. "My hat's off to you, Bertha. I don't know how you handle a big meal like this. I can barely manage soup in the crockpot. Much less a five-course meal."

"It's no big deal." Bertha looked embarrassed, but Kenzi suspected she was pleased. "You get used to it after a while. Chad helps some."

Jean made a scoffing noise. "Sure he does."

Chad sat up straight. "What's that supposed to mean?"

"I'm just wondering how you helped. Did you turn down the volume on the television so she could concentrate?"

"I'll have you know I help quite a bit around the house. Especially since...since..."

"Since you got laid off."

"I did not get laid off. Don't disrespect your parents."

"I'm not disrespecting my parentssss," she said, laying heavily on the s.

"Jean," Lionel said, "chill."

"I have a constitutionally protected right to speak my mind."

Chad's lips thinned. "Not at my table you don't."

"Is this your table? What makes it your table? Did you pay for it?"

"I made mortgage payments and kept the lights on for decades so you could have a home."

"Some home."

Chad rose. "What's wrong with our home? I think we have a fine home."

"And it's all about you, isn't it?" Jean also stood. "Did you ever ask Mother what she wanted? Did you ever ask if she thought we had a fine home?"

Lionel jumped to his feet. "Jean, calm down. You're ruining Christmas."

"Maybe it should be ruined."

"Says you. Because all you care about is yourself. Because you're a selfish, self-centered egomaniac. And you always have been."

Robert stood, reaching out. "I think everyone needs to get a grip on themselves."

"You would say that," Jean replied. "Is that a new car I saw in your driveway?"

"What's that got to do with anything?"

"Oh, nothing. My mother's necklace disappears. And you get a new car."

Robert appeared outraged. "Do you know how far back me and your papa go?"

"Yes," Jean said, "you two always work together, don't you?"

Even Bertha looked shocked. "Jean!"

"Are you going to take this too, Mother? Like you always lie down and take it?"

Bertha rose to her feet, but by this time, everyone was talking at once and Kenzi couldn't make out a word anyone was saying.

Sharon leaned over. Her eyes were wide and watery. "Kenzi, please stop this."

"What do you think I can do?"

"I don't know. You're smart. Think of something."

In fact, she did know how to interrupt this meltdown. She'd been planning to wait until later...but Sharon was right. This had to end before someone did some permanent damage.

She dodged hands and fists till she got to the kitchen. She let a few moments pass to make it seem less coincidental...

"I found it!"

Everyone at the table whirled around.

Kenzi stood in front of the swinging kitchen door. Holding a beautiful necklace with a luminescent pink teardrop pearl.

Bertha almost screamed. "You found it!"

"I did." She walked to the end of the table. Bertha reached for it, but Kenzi slid it over her neck. "This doesn't belong in a display case. This should be around your neck. Always."

"Where did you find it?"

"Under the refrigerator, believe it or not. I thought that cat of yours had a suspicious look on his face." She smiled. "I'm not sure where someone left it, but Gus thought it was another play toy. Probably batted it all over the house, until finally he knocked it under the fridge."

"And couldn't get it out. I never thought to look there." Tears welled up in Bertha's eyes. "I—I never thought I'd see this again. I was certain—" Her voice choked. "Doesn't matter." She looked across at her husband. "Chad, I guess you're going to have to put up with me a little longer."

"That will be my honor and privilege, sweet lady."

Sharon clapped her hands together. "Then you're not leaving, Mom?"

"Don't see how I can now." She looked at herself in the mirror. "I guess Christmas is the season of miracles."

AN HOUR LATER, everything and everyone had calmed down to such a dramatic extent that Kenzi began to think she'd imagined the open warfare she'd witnessed at the dinner table. The rest of the evening was peaceful, even joyous. After the table was cleared, everyone settled in the living room and more eggnog was poured. The tone was much more relaxed. Robert played carols on his harmonica. Lionel and Amanda tried to sing along, but they got lost somewhere around the seventh day of Christmas. Chad offered some holiday dance moves. Sharon and Jean actually hugged one another, like they meant it, and called each other "Sis" for the rest of the evening.

And Bertha was still wearing the necklace.

Just after ten, the guests started to depart. Jean, predictably, was the first. "I should go. Lots of work to do." She paused in front of Kenzi. "Thank you."

"Me? For what?"

"For reminding us what this holiday season is about. We will always have our differences. But at Christmas—we're a family." She stopped in front of her father. "Dad, I'm...sorry. About what I said. I didn't mean it."

He stood and hugged his eldest. "I know you didn't, sweetheart. We were just all so upset about that damned necklace."

"Blessed necklace," Bertha corrected. "I'm sure it makes no sense to anyone but me, but this necklace has become a validation. A symbol of continuity. Like the flag over the castle that tells everyone everything is still okay inside." She squeezed the pearl tightly. "I know I shouldn't put so much stock in...things."

"I can see how much better you are now that you have it back," Robert said, also rising. "It makes you happy."

"What makes me happy is this family. And that includes you, Robert."

"Aw shucks."

"It was so nice having you all together tonight. Let's do it again soon."

Robert followed Jean out the door. Lionel and Amanda were next to leave.

"I suppose we should go home too," Sharon said, yawning. "I bet Hailee is still awake, Kenzi. Probably hoping you'll let her get into her stocking before she goes to bed."

"No chance."

"I know, I know." Sharon gathered her coat, but just before they left, Kenzi placed a hand on her arm. "Sharon, would you mind starting the car? I'll be there in a minute."

"Too much eggnog?"

Kenzi smiled. "Out in a flash."

Sharon's mother walked her to the car, leaving Kenzi alone with Chad.

Kenzi spoke first. "It's Parkinson's, isn't it?"

Chad nodded slowly. "Early stages. But the doc says it's gonna get worse fast. Something called Parkinson's plus syndrome. Accelerates quickly, leads to dementia, and then..." He shook his head. "How did you know?"

Kenzi shrugged. "My grandmother had Parkinson's. I recognized the symptoms. When I saw your wife's hand trembling, that was the big giveaway. Plus she had trouble hearing. Diminished sense of smell. Trouble sleeping. And she mentioned that she'd seen a doctor recently."

"Of course you never know for sure." Just a look into Chad's eyes told Kenzi how much he loved his wife. "But she's only going to be able to enjoy a few more Christmases. Maybe... very few."

"So before it was too late, you wanted the whole family to gather for Christmas dinner. Because you knew nothing would mean more to your wife than that. But your children are busy adults with lives of their own. So how do you make that happen?" Kenzi smiled. "Make the symbolic linchpin of the marriage disappear. If that didn't bring the kids together, nothing would."

"I can see why Sharon likes you. You're smart."

"Nah. But I'm good at reading people. I worked as a counselor for a while and it gave me an understanding—and appreciation—of human nature. I wasn't convinced anyone here needed money badly enough to steal something that meant so much to your wife. But once I realized she was sick, and how much she wanted her family gathered together at Christmastime...I knew what must've happened."

"How did you find the necklace?"

"Oh, it wasn't hard, once I knew you were the one who made it disappear. I remembered what you said earlier about the privacy of your foot locker. So while you were all setting the table, I climbed into the attic and found it."

"I keep it locked."

"Yeah..." Kenzi's eyes rolled upward. "My sister Emma showed me how to pick locks. I keep a small pick on my keychain. It isn't tough when you know what you're doing. And that was an old lock."

"I knew losing the necklace would upset Bertha. But I thought it would be worth it if all the kids came over on Christmas Eve. And of course, I planned for it to miraculously reappear on the first day of Kwanzaa. When I saw the kids screaming at each other at the dinner table, I thought I'd made a horrible mistake. Thank goodness you were here to make everything right again." He paused. "And thanks for telling that story about the cat. Took the heat off me."

"I didn't want another Battle Royale. But you should tell your wife the truth."

"I will." He sighed. "Maybe not today."

"I don't think she'll be too angry. After all, you gave her what she wanted most. And she got the necklace back."

He nodded. "Once you get older, you realize how important family is. The only thing that matters, really. Especially at Christmastime."

"Right. Right." She paused, lost in thought. "Yeah. Especially at Christmastime."

∽

Kenzi stopped him just as he stepped outside the front door of his magnificent Mercer Island home.

"Kenzi! What a surprise!"

"Hi, *Papi*." She glanced at his wife. "Hello, Candice. You two on your way to church?"

Her father answered. "Of course. Midnight mass, like every other year. But I didn't expect—"

"Right. Neither did I."

"I didn't even think we were on speaking terms."

"Well, this isn't the office."

A car horn sounded in the street.

Her father peered into the night. "Is that...Emma?"

Kenzi grinned. "And Hailee. We even rounded up Gabe. You got the whole family tonight."

"But—But—" His voice choked. "Kenzi, I—I never—" He sniffed, cleared his throat. "I don't know what to say."

She wrapped her arm around his. "You don't have to say a word. Just get in the car and enjoy mass with your family. We're coming back tomorrow, too. I want to see what Santa brought you."

He wiped his hand across his eyes. "I already got the best possible gift. Merry Christmas, Kenzi."

She hugged him as close as she possibly could. "Merry Christmas, *Papi*."

ABOUT THE AUTHORS

Kenneth Andrus is a native of Columbus, Ohio. He obtained his undergraduate degree from Marietta College and his doctor of medicine from the Ohio State University College of Medicine. Following his internship, he joined the Navy and retired after twenty-four years of service with the rank of Captain. His operational tours while on active duty included: Battalion Surgeon, Third Battalion Fourth Marines; Brigade Surgeon, Ninth Marine Amphibious Brigade, Operation Frequent Wind; Medical Officer, USS *Truxtun* CGN-35; Fleet Surgeon, Commander Seventh Fleet; Command Surgeon, U.S. Naval Forces Central Command, Desert Shield/Desert Storm; and Fleet Surgeon, U.S. Pacific Fleet. His webpage can be found at: www.kennethandrus.com

William Bernhardt is the author of over fifty books, including *Splitsville (#1 National Bestseller)*, the historical novels *Challengers of the Dust* and *Nemesis*, two books of poetry, and the Red Sneaker books on writing. In addition, Bernhardt founded the Red Sneaker Writers Center to mentor aspiring authors. The Center hosts an annual conference (WriterCon), small-group seminars, a newsletter, and a bi-weekly podcast. Bernhardt has received the Southern Writers Guild's Gold Medal Award, the Royden B. Davis Distinguished Author Award (University of Pennsylvania) and the H. Louise Cobb Distinguished Author Award (Oklahoma State), which is given "in recognition of an outstanding body of work that has profoundly influenced the way in which we understand ourselves and American society at large." In 2019, he received the Arrell Gibson Lifetime Achievement Award from the Oklahoma Center for the Book.

Robert A. Brown has spent most of his working life in public education, serving as both a reading specialist and a principal, but he has also authored several nonfiction pieces dealing with the Great Depression and its popular culture, including western movies and the so-called "Spicy" magazines of the period. His work includes a piece on the legend of cowboy-movie star Tom Mix commissioned by the National Cowboy and Western Heritage Museum. An internationally known collector of nostalgic items such as movie paper, radio premiums, and pulp magazines, Brown supplied the art and wrote the text for Kitchen Sink Press's popular trading card series *Spicy: Naughty '30s Pulp Covers* and *Spicy: More Naughty '30s Pulp Covers*, which quickly became sold-out collector's items.

Tamara Grantham is the award-winning author of more than a dozen books and novellas, including the Olive Kennedy: Fairy World MD series, the Shine novellas, and the Twisted Ever After trilogy. *Dreamthief*, the first book of her Fairy World MD series, won first place for fantasy in INDIEFAB'S Book of the Year Awards, a RONE award for best New Adult Romance of 2016, and is a #1 bestseller on Amazon with over 200 five-star reviews. Tamara has been a featured speaker at numerous writing conferences and has been a panelist at Comic Con Wizard World. Born and raised in Texas, Tamara now lives with her husband and five children in Wichita, Kansas.

Betsey Kulakowski has thirty years of experience as an occupational safety professional and recently completed her degree in Emergency Management. She lives with her husband and two teenage children in Oklahoma. Betsey has been writing since she could, and created her first book at the age of six—cardboard cover, string binding and all.

John Wooley made his first professional sale in the late 1960s, placing a script with the legendary *Eerie* magazine. He's now in his sixth decade as a professional writer, having written three horror novels with co-author Ron Wolfe, including *Death's Door*, which was one of the first books released under Dell's Abyss imprint and was also nominated for a Bram Stoker Award. His solo horror and fantasy novels include *Awash in the Blood*, *Ghost Band*, and *Dark Within*, the latter a finalist for the Oklahoma Book Award. With Robert A. Brown he wrote the three novels in The Cleansing horror trilogy, *Seventh Sense*, *Satan's Swine*, and *Sinister Serpent*.

ALSO BY THE AUTHORS

Kenneth Andrus

The Defenders Thrillers

Flash Point

Amber Dawn

Arctic Meance

William Bernhardt

The Daniel Pike Legal Thriller Series

The Last Chance Lawyer

Court of Killers

Trial by Blood

Twisted Justice

Judge and Jury

Final Justice

The Splitsville Legal Thriller Series

Splitsville

Exposed

Shameless

Tamara Grantham

Never Call Me Vampire

The 7th Lie

Betsey Kulakowski

The Veritas Codex Series

The Veritas Codex

The Jaguar Queen

The Alien Accord

John Wooley and Robert A. Brown

The Cleansing Series

Seventh Sense

Satan's Swine

Sinister Serpent

John Wooley and Ron Wolfe

Old Fears

PUBLISHERS NOTE

Babylon Books is a division of Bernhardt Books, a family-owned publishing house founded in 1999 that specializes in showcasing emerging authors and compelling fiction.

Editor-in-Chief: Alice Bernhardt
Marketing Director: Ralph Bernhardt
Chief Financial Officer: Harrison Bernhardt

Made in the USA
Columbia, SC
18 December 2021

52092581R00131